D0712967

UNIVERS
PORTAG
WINNIPEG 2. MAN
CANADA
DISCARDED

# The Adventures of Captain Haylestone

# The Adventures of Captain Haylestone

by
Alan
Easton

McGRAW-HILL RYERSON LIMITED
Toronto Montreal New York London

THE ADVENTURES OF CAPTAIN HAYLESTONE



ISBN 0-07-082177-1

1 2 3 4 5 6 7 8 9 0 D 4 3 2 1 0 9 8 7 6 5

Printed and bound in Canada

For

*Sonia*

who knows the captain too.

# CARGO

1 The Girl from the Maritimes 1
2 The Barge 24
3 Cruising 39
4 The Foul Trophy 56
5 Rum Compass 73
6 Special Cargo 90
7 Pandemonium in the Cockpit 109
8 Loading Deep 127
9 Scuttling 144

# The Girl from the Maritimes

The sun came out from behind the white summer clouds and shone warmly on the backs of the two men leaning against the coaming of the fore hatch. Its rays also bore down on Captain Hiram Haylestone who was pacing the deck before them, the thick soles of his heavy boots striking the wooden planks with the sound of a horse backing out of its stall. The sunshine, not a common event in the port of Halifax, or on the Nova Scotia coast for that matter, did not radiate the joy it ought to have done among the officers of the *Maid of Jeddore*. A dark problem faced the captain which, if it were not solved, would descend on the mate and chief engineer and, in fact, on all hands.

The burden which the sun could not dispel was unemployment, the unemployment of the vessel. She had been lying idle alongside the wharf of her home port for almost two weeks now without even the prospect of a cargo. Captain Haylestone was open to transporting anything anywhere on the East Coast or even farther afield but maritime business seemed to have dried up.

"No outward freight," Haylestone rumbled as he made another turn.

Chief Engineer Angus McNiff was not sure that the temporary interruption of the little trader's passages was so vital. "You've had some pretty good voyages, Hiram," he said, looking up under his curious down-growing eyebrows at the tall, straight figure whose pacing was arrested by the remark. "You've made plenty. Time we had a holiday. For me, I'm glad to rest from the perpetual sweat and care of my engine."

Having made the statement McNiff put his bent cigarette back between his lips.

Haylestone glared down at the little man whose profession was emblazoned on his oily pants. "When did you sweat at your engine?" he barked. "All you have to do is turn a spigot, like on a rum keg, and the juice squirts into your diesel and it goes on running as long as the squirt lasts – or until I tell you to stop. Isn't that right, Merv?"

Mervin Quail, mate of the *Maid of Jeddore*, studied the wooden rail surmounting the bulwark.

"Isn't that so, Merv?" the captain repeated, his sharply pointed black beard jutting forward enquiringly.

The mate moved his heavy frame slightly and peered into the bowl of his pipe. "Well now," he said slowly. "Ask Angus, he'll know."

"That squirt as you call it requires tec . . . technology to make it work, and sweat, as I said before." McNiff pulled out his belt with a blackened thumb, deflated his portly front and tucked his carbonized undershirt more firmly into the aperture as though plugging a large pipe with asbestos packing. He gazed up at the strong, weather-beaten face. "You'll fetch a cargo again sometime, before it anywhere near hurts you. You just don't like being ashore; always want to be away at sea."

Captain Hiram Haylestone let his chief engineer's observation go and resumed his pacing.

He had come to own the handy little freighter several years before when she was put up for auction after spending the summer at Expo 67 where she had lain at the dock astern of the *Bluenose II*, representing a form of marine transport which, though declining, was still a lively business for those who knew the trade. She came on the market because her owners, Herman and Tanner of Lunenburg County, had departed this life in alphabetical order a little before the conclusion of Expo, owing, it was thought by some of the seafaring fraternity down East, to remaining too long in a port with such unfamiliar amenities as Montreal.

The vessel was a wooden double-ender – her stern was pointed like her bow – and she was just under 150 tons. She might have seemed a bit old-fashioned and lacking in modern scientific aids but these were not necessary to Captain Haylestone. Her length, 120 feet, just suited him.

For nearly thirty years he had plied the coastal routes but had recently lost his boat; some said that the customs had seized her but no one knew for certain. He put in a bid for the *Maid of the Mist* as she was then called and his tender was accepted. He changed her name when he registered her in Halifax, because he was not fond of fog, and mist was a reminder. Besides, there was a miserable little craft by the same name that fiddled about at the misty foot of Niagara Falls with tourists. He did not want any confusion with that boat, and since the late Mrs. Aggie Haylestone had come from East Jeddore, forty miles down the coast from Halifax, he felt it appropriate to name his new vessel in honour of her village. The other alteration he made was to lengthen the bunk in his cabin by eighteen inches.

Before taking delivery of the *Maid of Jeddore* he searched around for his old crew. They were vital to him, though neither Mate Mervin Quail nor Angus McNiff had ever been led to suppose so. He found Quail on a dredger in Halifax Harbour and McNiff in the sub-basement of the city gas plant. He tracked down the cook, a man who was invaluable in any sort of emergency as well as in the galley; and he located three of his former young seamen, Ed, Elmer and Ambrose. All downed tools when they got the call, like the disciples of an ancient prophet. He left the hiring of the second engineer to McNiff; he had no wish to be responsible for the selection of an assistant to Chief Engineer Angus McNiff.

Captain Haylestone had done quite well with the *Maid of Jeddore* in those four years. Operations had been mainly on the East Coast; lobsters from Labrador, cattle from Prince Edward Island, sometimes trips to the West Indies for rum. But all this fine trade seemed to have come to an end. Today he paced his deck in desolating uncertainty.

Suddenly a small bus-like vehicle, which had been cruising down the wharf at a speed in excess of the limit proclaimed by the Harbour Board, swivelled round and brought up abreast of the *Maid of Jeddore*. Its door opened and slammed behind a dapper-looking type who stepped over the ditch between the dock and the boat, there being no gangplank, and dropped lightly from the rail onto the fore deck.

"You must be the captain," he said at once, his hand outstretched. He could hardly mistake who was in command. The tarnished gold laurel leaves were still evident on Haylestone's salt-encrusted cap; the once gold stripes on his reefer jacket were quite visible. Besides, his height made him the first man anyone would notice.

"Yes," said Haylestone, his hand closing like a vice over the visitor's.

"I'm Algernon Forsyth. You are Captain Haylestone I believe. You busy?"

"Busy? Yes. Always busy," Haylestone retorted eyeing the man's liberally chequered clothes.

"Have you a few minutes?"

"Depends what you want."

"I have a proposition to make, Captain. Can we discuss it somewhere?"

"In that case you'd better come to my cabin."

Leaving Angus McNiff with a disappointed expression and Merv Quail standing without the support of the hatch coaming, the captain led the way off the fore deck, up the ladder to the bridge and through the wheel-house into his small cabin behind it.

"Have a seat on the settee Mr. . . . Forsyth. What's your proposition?" Haylestone always came to the point without palaver – unless negotiations were tricky and called for the indirect technique.

Mr. Forsyth looked up brightly. "I'm with the CBC, Captain. Television producer. We're filming a play and I want some shots on the water. One episode involves a small ship and yours seems the most suitable."

"Oh," Haylestone murmured.

"Can you take my party out for a few days?"

"Take your party out!" Haylestone searched the man's round smooth face surmounted by abundant grey wavy hair worked into the back of his neck.

"Just around the coast a bit."

Haylestone reached into his shirt pocket and pulled out a White Owl. "This isn't a passenger ship. I have no license for the carriage of passengers." He lit his cigar with a large match which he struck on the sole of his boot.

"No. It would just be two or three day-trips. Out in the morning if the weather is favourable for shooting, back in the evening. Surely there's no need for a license for that."

"There is. But I couldn't get one for this vessel. Have to have life saving equipment and all that. The *Maid of Jeddore* is a coastal freighter."

"I know." Mr. Forsyth was a blithe spirit. "But these technicalities could be circumvented, I expect."

Captain Haylestone was not unfamiliar with circumvention. Such a suggestion drew him instinctively towards Mr. Forsyth and the CBC. He took the offensive.

"Mr. Forsyth. As I said, this is a freighter." He chewed on his cigar and gazed out the port hole for a moment as though searching for something. "I'm waiting momentarily for a cargo. It isn't here yet but it may be at any time. Now supposing I weren't here when it arrived, the cargo would be lying on the wharf and costing me a packet to keep it there. The economics of operating a freighter calls for sailing close hauled all the time you know."

Mr. Forsyth frowned. "It might not arrive though."

"It could. You never know. These shippers are as uncertain as the post office."

"That means it'll be delivered late. The cost would probably be a bagatelle, anyway. I think we could compensate you for any commercial loss."

Being fairly satisfied thus far Haylestone asked how many were in his crew.

"Only four besides myself. My two cameramen and H.B. and Meg, who have the principal roles. I want to take them out to film the sea a bit and the shore and try out a few sequences. If all works out well, I'll go into production with the full cast – on shore of course."

Hiram Haylestone was not one to leave the end of a new rope unspliced. "Rum, Mr. Forsyth?"

"I'd be obliged."

Lifting one end of the settee cushion and removing a trapdoor he pulled out a large bottle of dark red liquid labeled Schreecher's and poured a liberal quantity into two glasses. "Here's to the CBC," he said.

Mr. Forsyth stood up, took a draught, coughed and felt his way down to the settee again.

"I suppose," said Haylestone, "we should consider the freightage, that is, the terms. You had better take the *Maid of Jeddore* under charter – just verbal charter will do – so much per day including mid-day dinner in the mess-room."

"That's satisfactory."

"Let's see then. Allowance for contingencies; if weather's unsuitable charges go on; insurance against early arrival of cargo. And, of course, risk: taking passengers without a license. Expensive danger that." The captain took another drink and wiped his long up-swept moustache.

"How would $800 a day suit you, Captain?"

"$800?"

It was not very difficult for Captain Haylestone to persuade Mr. Forsyth to jack it up to $1,500 after talking about the merits of the CBC and other pleasant things. To the captain it was a matter of waiting for a friend to take his cough medicine until he could speak comfortably. And Forsyth seemed quite happy about it, claiming he really didn't know anything much concerning freightage. The deal was concluded, the charter to commence as of 6 a.m. the next day.

At nine o'clock in the morning the *Maid of Jeddore* was passing out of the harbour with the sun, once more kind, glinting on the rippled water. Captain Hiram Haylestone stood on his bridge outside the wheel-house with the mate contemplating the soot belching from the thin black funnel.

"Angus McNiff always seems to do that when he starts. Fouling up the deck, damn him! Should clean out his engine more often."

Mervin Quail grunted.

The passengers, who were standing in the bow rejoicing in the sights and sounds of the sea, were probably unaware of the oily carbon raining down on their fancy clothes.

"Profitable cargo, Merv," Haylestone said brightly. There was no immediate response. "Profitable cargo."

The mate gazed forward and shifted his pipe to the other side of his mouth. "Don't know but what you ain't right, Hiram."

The party's rapture left them when they came abeam of Chebucto Head and felt the heave of the Atlantic swell. They lay down on the hatch or, worse, reclined in the mess-room adjoining the galley. But it was only for a matter of three hours. At 12.30 they nosed into Mahone Bay. Sheltered by the Tancooks all was peace again, the calm blue water stretching for five miles before them dotted here and there with small islands.

Algernon Forsyth said no one wanted lunch, work would do them more good. He marshalled his crew on the fore deck and while the two photographers set up their cameras, he had the leading actor, called H.B. Smith for some reason, a good-looking, clean shaven young man, stand in different positions and voice a few words and display his white enamelled teeth frequently. Meg Myles arranged herself in pleasing attitudes which Haylestone, on the bridge above while the vessel glided gently over the water, thought charming. To see well-cut summer slacks clinging to the thigh of a girl standing in the lee of the winch on his own vessel was a prettier picture than any cruise-ship poster he had ever seen. Merv Quail, though given somewhat to brevity, did remark that she was a knockout.

The cameramen took shots of the two of them talking together and singly. Quail offered his assistance in laying ropes in suitable places and producing an axe and a couple of marline spikes to help the effects – props they called them. When asked for a deck-chair he had to admit they had none but he fetched the collapsible stool from the wheel-house which the captain sometimes used. He was even photographed helping Meg Myles onto the hatch.

Haylestone took the *Maid* close inshore so that pictures could be taken of the rocks and beaches. Altogether it had been a busy afternoon and by five Mr. Forsyth decided to pack up. They would have their lunch now he said, if it was all right with the captain. It was more a matter of whether it was all right with the cook, which it was.

But there was a delay. Haylestone felt they deserved a drink which he was quite prepared to supply *gratis.* They sat around the mess-room table, the only place for convivial conversation, and drank to the making of *The Girl from the Maritimes*, and several other things. As Forsyth had decided that they would not return to Halifax that evening but would spend the night at the town of Mahone Bay, the party was freed from the prospect of the rolling voyage back.

The CBC did not embark until ten o'clock the next morning which annoyed Haylestone because his vessel was readily noticeable at the Mahone Bay dock and the legality of the transport of passengers still weighed on his mind when in possible sight of even minor officials. But his discomfort seemed to leave him when he saw Meg Myles gliding down the wharf. He cast off and steered out into the bay as soon as they were all on board.

They were very pleased with yesterday's pictures. The films had been sent to Halifax for processing and returned with the sound track synchronized. Forsyth and the senior cameraman were particularly impressed with Merv Quail's photogenic qualities. The films showed him to be the true, intrepid sailor, the stuff heroes were supposed to be made of, but he was short on sound.

The weather had reverted to its usual form, dull with a fog bank on the horizon. Forsyth wanted to get close in to a beach again and Haylestone selected Shoal Cove across the bay. In an hour they had reached the bell buoy on the ten-fathom line opposite the cove. There the director asked him to stop. Some discussion took place among the party. Presently they broke up and Forsyth came up to the bridge while a camera was being set up in the bow.

"Will you go in as near as you can to the beach, Cap?" Forsyth asked.

"What do you mean by near?"

"A hundred yards or so maybe."

"Can't go in to a hundred yards with this vessel. Might get in to two hundred."

"That'll probably do," Forsyth agreed and went down.

Haylestone put the engine room telegraph to half speed. The ring of acknowledgement came at once and a slight throb passed through the boat. He leaned over the bridge rail and shouted for the mate.

Quail appeared from the neighbourhood of the principal protagonists.

"Stand by the anchor, Merv, in case we need it," the captain told him. "And have Elmer get the lead out and take soundings from the weather bow. We're going close in to the beach there."

The cameraman was soon trying to dodge the lead as the seaman swung the heavy weight at the end of the line. There was plenty of water: seven fathoms.

Haylestone glanced at the beach, estimating the distance, and then watched the men in the bow for a few moments. The second cameraman – though it was difficult to distinguish between the two because they were both abundantly bearded – seemed to be taking shots of Elmer and Merv Quail. He carried his camera on a sort of shoulder rest. It was curious how . . .

Something on the fore deck diverted his attention. Meg Myles, who had been attractively dressed when she came aboard, was walking forward, making towards the forecastle, clad only in her underwear, that is, she seemed to be wearing what to the best of his knowledge were known as panty hose, and a bra. No slacks! No sweater! Haylestone had admired Meg, and the others had held her in high esteem, not to say admiration. What was this?

He vaguely heard Elmer intoning the depth of water, "By the deep four. By the mark three." He looked away, embarrassed, then he peered down on the deck again. Meg had passed the scuttle leading down into the forecastle and was approaching the senior cameraman. The male lead was following her closely along the deck. She would come within eyeshot of Merv in a moment. If the leadsman saw her and was distracted . . .

Haylestone glanced shorewards. He now saw boulders and jagged rocks protruding from the yellow sand. They stood out as clearly as Meg Myles had a moment ago, but unlike that vision they were positively ugly.

His eyes came back to focus on the leadsman. "Sounding, Elmer. What's your sounding?" His voice echoed from the low cliff behind the beach.

"Stop engines," he roared to the man at the wheel a few feet away with almost the same force. The telegraph jangled.

It was Quail who answered. Hearing the strident voice he jumped to the rail – he was capable of swift movement when haste was called for – and noted the leadsman's line. "By the mark two . . . Two, Hiram . . . Mark two," he shouted urgently.

There was a sudden jerk. Haylestone was unbalanced for a moment and thrown, though not heavily, against the rail in front of him.

"Hell! Blast! By thunder! . . . Full astern." That yell also echoed. "What have you got now Merv?"

"By the mark two less a half."

"Fathom and a half!" Haylestone muttered. "Nine feet. Damn my bloody buttons!"

He leapt into the wheel-house in four strides, seized the telegraph handle and threw it back and forth winding up with a bang on the arrester knob at full astern. "If Angus doesn't give her full power now I'll go below and do it myself!"

It was as well Angus was not present. Ed, who was at the wheel, crouched out of the way.

Swinging outside again, he addressed Quail in the same voice. "Keep the lead on the bottom, Merv, and let me know when the line leads back. She's aground."

That phrase was one of the worst that a shipmaster could utter. Captain Hiram Haylestone's heart felt like a hunk of ballast.

Then an extraordinary phenomenon caught his eye. Someone was swimming, swimming towards the shore. Surely no one was abandoning ship! Up in the bow Algernon Forsyth seemed to be giving directions to the cameraman as he and the male lead leaned forward watching intently. The cranker was bent at his machine and appeared to be looking through a telescope or something. Meg Myles was not to be seen. Then a word he had heard shot into his mind. Script. They had said things were in the script.

"She's stuck fast," came the hail from Quail. "Lead line's leading up and down."

The racing propeller was shaking the stern like a duck throwing water off its tail and the vibration rattled the rigging. But the bow where the photography was going on was steady, secured to the sandy bottom.

The second engineer's head appeared at the top of the ladder. "Skipper. Mr. McNiff wants to know what's the matter."

The captain swung round. "What! Tell Mr. McNiff to mind his own bloody business and drive his engine astern until he breaks the piston rods."

The second's head receded from view.

By this time the swimmer was coming back. She knew how far she had to go to be out of range of the camera. The sequence of her coming through the surf and beaching herself, like the *Maid,* would be taken later from the shore. Now Meg had to be rescued.

"Will you have a ladder dropped over the side, Cap," Algernon Forsyth called up to the bridge. "Meg's nearly back."

"Forsyth, you idiot!" was all Algernon heard. But Ambrose, a smart able seaman, got a rope ladder and threw it over.

Meg's lovely teeth were chattering when she reached the deck. The male lead wrapped her in a duffel coat and took her to the warm galley. The cook said she could change in the mess-room and he would provide a towel and tea and guard the door.

After some shouted discussion between the captain on the bridge and the mate at the bow with the lead line showing no sign of running out as the propeller ploughed astern, Haylestone decided to give it up. He stopped the engine.

"How's the tide? That's what we've got to find out," Haylestone said to Quail when he came up to the wheel-house. "Tide tables. Tide tables. Ah, here they are." He found them among his nautical books in his cabin.

"Ain't much rise and fall here, Hiram."

"Five feet or so, I guess. Let's see. Mahone Bay." Haylestone's wetted thumb flicked over the pages. "July. Yes, neaps. Says here . . . look at this, Merv. Says, 'high tide 9.20 pm. Height 4.6 feet'. That means it's low water a bit before four. Falling tide now." He looked at the clock on the after bulkhead. "Half past twelve. By eight this evening the flood tide should be lifting her."

"But you don't know how hard she's im . . . imbedded," Quail argued.

"No. Maybe stuck as tight as the engine when Angus seized it up that time. On the other hand . . . "

The captain put the book down and gazed out the wheel-house window as though he could see the stem up on the shelving sand. Then he swung round. "We'll kedge her off, Merv. Can't take the chance of her floating off."

The mate moved out through the door, looked aft, clutched his pipe and puffed and came back. "Yeah. Kedge her off."

"Glad you agree, Merv. Get to work right away." Haylestone could leave it to Quail now, he was first class when it came to practical seamanship.

The hands began hauling ropes aft, the kedge anchor was unlashed, and there was clattering on the boat deck. The cook reluctantly left the guardianship of the mess-room when called aloft to remove his vegetables from cold storage in the starboard life-boat. The number two cameraman seemed to be practicing his art by filming whatever he saw.

When they put the boat in the water it leaked considerably but not more than was to be expected of a little used boat. The male lead appointed himself master-bailer.

They led the rope out the stern and slung the anchor beneath the boat and, with the male lead and the cook bailing, Meg now being on deck attired in her slacks and sweater, they rowed out about a hundred yards and dropped the kedge. When they returned they hoisted the boat to avoid bailing.

At seven o'clock they hauled the heavy rope taut and put a strain on it. The vessel did not move. At fifteen minute intervals Quail pressed the windlass to the utmost of its capacity but she did not come off. Haylestone, who had been easy about the whole matter until half past eight, an hour or so before high water, now became worried. He told the chief engineer to stand by to drive his engine astern as hard as he could.

At nine, with roughly half an hour to go and still daylight enough to see what took place, Quail put a breaking strain on the kedge rope and Haylestone ordered full speed astern.

The vibration was shocking. Then the engine stopped, seemingly of its own accord, but the rope came in on the windlass.

She unplugged.

They hauled out to the kedge and picked it up and Haylestone put the engine room telegraph to slow astern to get farther out – but nothing happened. There was no answering ring.

As he stepped out of the wheel-house he almost ran the chief down. McNiff was out of breath. Glaring down at him Haylestone wanted to know what he was doing on the bridge. But he knew it was something vital or he would not have been there.

"Propeller's loose," McNiff panted. "Banging like hell."

"Loose! Propeller? Can't be!"

"Is. Can't turn it way it is."

"How loose?"

"Bloody loose I'd say."

"Yes. She shook just now enough to bring down the topmast."

"It was your working her astern so hard, Hiram. That's what it was." McNiff had recovered enough for a longer statement.

"You're the one who's turning the shaft," Haylestone roared. "You know how much the screw will take. You probably jerked it."

"Jerked it! You might as well say I kicked it."

"Pin must have sheared and the nut started to come off the tail-end shaft. Could only do that going astern."

Haylestone looked about him. He glanced at the beach in the fading light. Then he applied his mind to McNiff again.

"Go down and put her slow ahead. I'll try to turn her around. Got to get into deeper water."

"Turn the screw! It'll fall off likely as not if I do."

"Going ahead will tend to screw the nut on. Can't go astern again as I'd like to; the nut would come right off probably. Then we'd lose it on the bottom – and the propeller. Bronze propeller. Can't afford to drop that."

McNiff wiped his face with a rag he pulled out of his pants pocket, the outcome of habit in the engine room, then stared up at the captain. But it was difficult to tell where he was actually looking because of his curious eyebrows; he gave the impression of peering through a cedar hedge. "Bad business," he muttered at last.

"Well, don't stand there like that stupid boy on the burning deck. We'll be aground again with the flood tide if we don't get clear quick."

"Aground again!" McNiff felt for the ladder rail. "Okay, Hiram, I'll do what I can." Loyalty always unaccountably forged its way through when his captain was in dire straits – but the straits had to be pretty dire. He backed down the ladder and was gone.

In a few moments Haylestone felt the propulsion and put the wheel hard aport. Slowly the bow swung around and the captain steered for the bell buoy which now displayed its red flashing light. It was dark by the time the stricken vessel was safely clear and had her anchor down.

The *Maid of Jeddore* might as well have been in the Arctic as in Mahone Bay. It was ten miles across to the town wharf she had left this morning but Hiram Haylestone felt he could not risk making the passage for repairs, short as it was. He called the mate and the chief engineer up to his cabin.

"What you going to do, Hiram?" McNiff asked impatiently.

"Tip her," Haylestone announced without hesitation.

"Yeah. Where?"

"Here."

"Here!" exclaimed the chief. "Tip her here!"

"That's what I said."

Merv Quail took off his cap and scratched his head. His mouth was slightly ajar. Then he said, "Spare-me-days!"

McNiff felt for his cigarette papers. "Why don't you get her towed over to Mahone where it's safe to tip her."

"And what do you think a tug would cost, if I could get one? Can't afford that sort of luxury. You know what hard times we've had; no money in the kitty. How are your pumps, Angus?"

"Pumps? Ain't nothing wrong with them."

"Merv. We'll put hoses down the fore hold and get enough water into her to put her bow down and cock her stern up."

Quail's forehead creased. "Yeah. Could do that there."

"If we can expose the tail-end shaft Angus'll be able to get at the nut with his big spanner and tighten it up."

"Me?" McNiff questioned "Suspended from a rope over the stern getting pneumonia! You must be out of your mind, Hiram."

"We'll see," Haylestone said. "Now Merv, get the hoses down and pump the water in."

Quail hoisted himself to his feet. "What do we do with them CBC people?" he asked.

"Yes, I've been thinking about them," Haylestone said. "By cripes! If I hadn't taken them, I wouldn't be in this lousy position."

Quail offered to give up his cabin to the girl. He spoke briefly of Meg's merits as a brave swimmer and McNiff said he was sorry he hadn't witnessed the feat and felt she hadn't received sufficient recognition for her heroic deed. Haylestone said it was no more heroic than Angus going over the stern; it was just part of the job, actress or marine engineer.

With that they all went below, Quail to the hoses with his men, McNiff to his dungeon aft and Haylestone to the mess-room where he found the CBC being attended to by the cook.

Forsyth was indeed very understanding about the whole affair and his party seemed quite happy to bed down anywhere for the night. In fact, the cook had already made the arrangements – along the lines he knew would be approved by the captain. Haylestone said they must have a drink to help them forget the comfortable quarters ashore of which they were being deprived. The cook poured ample slugs of Schreecher's from a bottle he had taken the liberty of removing from the captain's cabin to revive Miss Myles after her valiant swim, but there was hardly enough to go round so he replenished it with another, and later another.

All were very jovial and they missed the captain every time he went out on deck to check with Merv Quail the effect of the water ballast on the vessel's trim, and they cheered him when he came back. Songs were sung, conducted by the male lead. Angus McNiff was present, having been drawn there, he said, from the necessity of having to fortify himself against the rigours he might be exposed to the next day. He was wearing his new sharply creased drip-dry pants, held in a position low down on his torso by his best belt with the fleur-de-lis buckle he always claimed to have won on the river ice at the Quebec winter carnival. Merv Quail came in at frequent intervals, said nothing, but had a happy smile more or less continuously and particularly for Meg Myles when she sang.

Water was still pouring into the fore hold and the bow was going deeper when dawn came up. Soon after nine it was judged that the stern was high enough and the hoses were shut off.

Merv Quail was the first to examine the condition of the propeller. They lowered him down over the stern on a bos'un's chair until he reached its centre. He found the nut behind the propeller had worked back on the thread of the shaft about two turns. He did some tapping with a heavy hammer and was then hauled up to review his diagnosis with the captain and chief engineer.

Curiosity seemed to have gripped the CBC. They were stretching their necks over the taffrail but could not see much because the aperture was under the counter. Forsyth asked if he could have the life-boat to watch the operation from the water because it might give them an idea for *The Girl from the Maritimes*. Haylestone was pretty short with him but said he could have it if the seamen could lower it in their present awkward trim. But they must provide the bailing personnel.

Haylestone decided that Quail and McNiff should go down on separate bos'un's chairs and work together; it was a job demanding both strength, which Quail had, and the skill and experience of a man accustomed to screwing nuts onto bolts.

McNiff did not view the latter requirement with the same degree of importance. "Send one of them sailors down; Ed's a smart hand."

"No," Haylestone argued, "it needs an engineer."

"I'll send the second engineer," McNiff said.

Like a choir master, Haylestone could detect a faulty note in the vocalist through long acquaintance. "That job demands an engineer with a chief's certificate. I don't want any five-eight fitter playing around with my propeller so it'll drop off the tail end when I'm least expecting it."

The end of McNiff's yellowing cigarette quivered like an aspen. "I told you before, Hiram, chief engineers operate inboard."

The captain leaned forward. "Angus McNiff, that's a lot of balony. Did you ever hear of a constipated seagull?"

"N . . . no. Not them birds."

"Nor did I; any more than I've heard of a chief who wouldn't drop over the stern to screw a nut on his tail end."

The chief looked at the taffrail. Haylestone said that if he fell off his perch, he was sure Meg Myles would dive in and rescue him before he drowned.

The seamen were very helpful in fixing McNiff into his chair, rather like a dentist and his nurse settling a man down before pulling a molar. The chief and the mate eventually reached the exact position below, and the large spanner and a bag of tools were lowered on a rope. Unfortunately, by this time there was a lop on the water and the cold sea periodically surrounded McNiff's short lower members. Colourful hues encircled his feet from the oil that oozed from his shoes. Quail was wisely wearing his long rubber boots.

With encouragement from the stalwart Quail, who did most of the hammering to drive the propeller home, and with the close attention he had to pay to the nut and his safety, McNiff did not notice what the boat's crew were doing. In fact, he was merely aware that the boat was there and felt more secure because of its presence.

It took them nearly an hour, McNiff calling the nut all kinds of things. When they were hauled up on deck, Quail, acknowledging all was now well, went off to get the life-boat hoisted. McNiff ordered the second to start the pumps and then descended to the warm engine room to get the circulation back into his legs and feet. He was soon followed by the cook who brought him something of what was left over from the night before.

Algernon Forsyth said they would stay overnight again at Mahone and would be ready to sail back to Halifax the next day if the sea was calm. It was not until the late afternoon that the *Maid of Jeddore* was pumped dry and ready to make the bay crossing. But in the interval Algie Forsyth had not wasted time.

His cameramen had taken shots of the sky over Great Tancook Island; the sea, which had roughened somewhat; gulls in flight and at rest. Cameras whirred while Meg and H.B. Smith leaned against the bulwark and talked in some kind of exotic script dialogue. For fun, it seemed, they took Captain Haylestone on the bridge with Elmer at the wheel, and then went down to the engine room and took McNiff lubricating. Coming across the bay they hung over the bow and cranked at the water splashing from the stem.

When the party came aboard in the morning, Captain Haylestone was tied up with a representative of the explosives division of the C.I.L. When the conference was over he came down to the mess-room where the mate and chief were drinking coffee with the CBC. Haylestone reluctantly told Forsyth that he could not take him back because of urgent business.

"I'm going to stay in Mahone Bay for a couple of days."

"You can't do that at this stage, Cap," Forsyth protested. "I want to return now and do some filming on the way."

Haylestone explained he had just concluded a contract to pick up a load of dynamite at the Oakland wharf a mile across the inlet for the mines in Newfoundland. It was just luck that the *Maid of Jeddore* had been in Mahone Bay when a boat was needed at the dynamite terminal.

Forsyth was obviously annoyed. He scrutinized his coffee as though it were sulphur and molasses.

Meg, in her bright way, asked him to reveal the conclusions he had come to at the hotel. "Do Algie dear. It's terribly exciting and I'm sure it will persuade Captain Haylestone to change his plans for today."

Algie turned his attention to the ketchup and pickle rack on the bulkhead and went on thinking.

"You know, Captain," Meg pursued, "last night we screened the rushes – the films we took yesterday – and your crew was tremendous. You were superb. Angus was out of this world sitting on the propeller and down with his engine. Merv, the strong silent mate, was wonderful. What do you say now Algie?" she asked.

But it wasn't Algie who had anything to say, it was a visitor who appeared at the mess-room door. Haylestone recognized him to be a member of the port authority. Knowing the breed, the captain left the mess-room for the fresh air of the deck and to gain manoeuvreability.

"I'm Simmons, the harbour master," said the man when they got outside."

"I know. We've met before."

"You been sailing out of here with passengers."

"Sailing out of here with . . . You coming aboard telling me . . . You'd better come up to my cabin and I'll put you straight on what might seem to be what it isn't."

Haylestone's cabin sometimes provided even greater freedom for manoeuvre than the deck. Seating his guest at one end of the settee and lifting the trapdoor at the other he remarked that he didn't see why they should have to wait for the sun to get any nearer the meridian. Filling the two glasses to a level somewhat above the midriff of the engraved mermaids, he handed one to Mr. Simmons.

"Schreecher's. Good when neat. You know the stuff as well as I do."

"Sure do," Simmons said taking a good swig. He did not cough but he soon spoke. "These passengers you've had aboard . . . "

"You mean the people you saw in the mess-room?"

"Yes."

"Seem to be a nice lot. CBC gang it seems. Want me to take them to Halifax. Stupid idea. I'm going across to Oakland for dynamite presently."

"But yesterday you were out with . . . "

"Is that dynamite wharf a good one to moor to?"

"Why, yes."

"I haven't got a chart of this part of the bay."

"You should have. Now, Capt'n, what about those passengers you've been carrying?"

"I don't really need a chart. Mahone Bay, like the whole coast, is laid out like a picture in my head . . . Here, let me fill up the boiler as we used to say in the days of steam."

"Thanks, Capt'n." Simmons held out his glass. "Now, about those . . . what do you call 'em, CBC artists?"

"Here's to the port of Mahone Bay. You're harbour master of Oakland too?"

"Oh, yes . . . You often take passengers?"

"Passengers? I just got through telling you these people you saw in the mess-room *asked* me to take them to Halifax but I refused, flatly refused.

"Oh," Simmons murmured. Then he leaned forward. "I thought you did . . . did carry them."

"The *Maid of Jeddore* isn't equipped to take passengers. You must know that. If this was a passenger ferry I'd probably be that distracted I'd run aground or get involved in a collision."

"Ah, yes." The harbour master held his glass up to the light and examined the mermaid. Then he emptied it.

"Well, I guess I'll have to be pushing off to the dynamite wharf," said Haylestone with finality. "And see that gang down below ashore."

"Yes. You'll find it a good wharf," Simmons said as they went down on deck. "May see you over there tomorrow."

A nice easy fellow, Haylestone thought, as he watched him making his way up the dock.

Algie Forsyth was in good spirits when the captain returned to the mess-room. He stood up and tugged at the bottom front of his sweater as thought it were a vest.

"Say, Cap. We could go over to this dynamite terminal and film the loading of a dangerous cargo."

"If you go round by road and get permission to go in," said Haylestone.

"We'll do that. As Meg said a while ago we had some fine shots yesterday – and the day before. We could get some more today. Altogether I think we have the makings of a most successful TV drama. *The Girl from the Maritimes* will come to life: ship laden with dynamite runs aground on a lonely island, near loss of propeller, magnificent seamanship, leaking life-boats to the rescue, and girl swims ashore . . . better have an explosion. Yes, *The Girl's* in the bag."

# The Barge

The seas which had tossed the *Maid of Jeddore* for two days and almost uprooted her deck-house had subsided. She no longer slid down between the jagged, foam-streaked waves and swung up over their breaking crests. The hurricane that had lashed the little wooden vessel had blown itself out; the strain on her deeply laden hull had been eased, her cargo still intact. Only an oily undulation spoke of the storm that had gone before.

Captain Hiram Haylestone leaned over the chart table in his small cabin abaft the wheel-house, working out his position from his observations of the fitful October sun. He did not care much for celestial navigation; he preferred visual piloting on the coast. But he had had to use his old sextant this voyage, which had taken him to Jamaica for a cargo of rum. He was just about to subtract the sun's declination from the zenith distance when the mate's voice interrupted his calculation.

"Barge on the starboard bow," Mervin Quail announced.

The captain jerked his tall body upright. "What do you see?" he inquired sharply. "Barge?"

As they went out Haylestone picked his peaked cap off the door knob and pushed it onto his black-thatched head.

"You're right, Merv. Barge all right. But what's it doing out here three hundred miles from the coast?

Big fellow too. Starboard," Haylestone ordered the man at the wheel and then rang the engine room telegraph to 'slow.'

They manoeuvred within fifty yards of the craft and stopped.

It was a beautiful steel barge about 200 feet long – longer by 80 feet than the *Maid of Jeddore*. It was black and fairly freshly painted, though white-streaked here and there with salt. It had a red bottom which they could see as it wallowed uncontrolled in the slow, heaving swell.

"Looks like she's got a full load of cargo," observed Haylestone. "She's lying pretty deep in the water. No identification on her this side, eh? We'll go round her. Her port of registry will be on the stern."

But it was not. The only marks she had were six cryptic numerals painted in white on her bow and stern, which meant nothing.

Captain Haylestone looked carefully round the horizon then contemplated the slow corkscrew motion of the barge again, trying to assess its value, excluding whatever cargo might be inside it. Slowly drawing a slim package of White Owls from an inner packet, not taking his eyes off the object of interest, he bit off the end of a cigar and struck a large match.

"We'll take it in tow, Merv," he suddenly announced.

"I was just about thinking the same thing, Hiram. But, spare-me-days, it'll be dirty boarding it from the boat."

"You can do it all right. Get the hands along."

The three deck hands and the cook rowed over the swell with Quail at the tiller and a light line trailing. It was a hard pull and as hard a task to board the barge. Elmer missed it once, but they fished him out and emptied his sea-boots. Mervin Quail made an inspection of the craft but there was nothing on the flush deck to indicate even where the barge was built. The four manhole doors were secured with many bolts. Oil, Quail thought. They hauled over the largest ropes and secured them to the main bollards, around one of which they noticed the remnants of a hawser; then they left precariously and rowed back.

As Captain Hiram Haylestone got under way with his tow, he ordered the mate to go down the fore hold and broach one of the cases of cargo, bring up two bottles and put them in the mess-room catsup and pickle rack. The boat's crew, he said, deserved a refresher.

Twilight fell on the gently tumbling sea with the *Maid of Jeddore* pulling hard. Captain Haylestone stood in the wing of the bridge keenly observing the behaviour of his hawsers as they stretched and gave in response to the influence of the waves. His concentration was suddenly interrupted by Angus McNiff, the chief engineer, who was talking loudly to himself as he mounted the ladder. He must have been helping the men in the mess-room to splice the main brace, as Haylestone thought the navy called it. The moment he reached the top step he launched into recriminations without a break in his self-conversation.

" . . . and I'll tell the skipper . . . Ah . . . I'll tell you Hiram, you'll be doing imitable damage . . . illitable . . . illimitable damage to my engine if you persist in trying to make full speed. Fit to blow all joints in the cylinder head, it is. And what's more . . . "

"What are you bellowing about, Angus. You know quite well . . . "

"And what's more . . . "

"You know quite well," Haylestone roared down at the stout little man who was carrying a stiltson wrench, "it makes no difference to the engine what weight it's pulling. We just go slower, that's all."

"What's more, you've bust my utility hoist."

"Your what?"

"Utility hoist." McNiff laboriously knocked the ash off his home-made cigarette with an oily finger.

"Never heard of such a thing."

"You were heaving your tow rope in on the utility hoist and stripped it."

"Are you talking about a winch, Angus?"
"Of course."
"Well why don't you call it a ruddy winch."
"Utility hoist," retorted the chief engineer. He grasped the rail and looked back at the barge. From behind, with the seat of his pants sagging down towards the back of his knees, Haylestone thought he looked rather like a dog standing on his hind legs. "Too heavy to tow," he added.
"Whenever I have a bit of luck and am doing something worthy of the *Maid* you come and turn the hose on it."
A seagull flew low and cried out, which seemed to irritate McNiff still more. He scowled at the bird as he followed it in the dying light through his down-growing eyebrows. "How far are you going with it?"
"Home."
"You going to take it home!"
"Sure. Where else?"
"Why don't you take it to the nearest port in the States? I may not have fuel for the job."
"Because there's no American port nearer; that's one reason why. And don't talk to me about fuel; you've got plenty. Come in and look at the chart if you want," he added more convivially. The captain's appeasement tactics when the chief was in his moods always had to be accompanied by good timing. But it was nearly spoiled now when McNiff was ordered to leave his wrench outside the wheel-house because of the compass.
"Deep water out here," Haylestone indicated with a massive finger circling a spot on the chart. "Delaware Bay is a good three hundred miles away and the Bay of Fundy about the same. As we're going there, that's where we'll take the barge."
A tapping was heard beneath their feet. It was the cook signalling the second sitting for supper. There was a worn spot above the galley stove where the cook had called the captain to meals with his cleaver for years.

"Salvage is a luxury we seldom come by," Haylestone said as they were going down. "They pay good money for salvage, and for all we know that barge has gold in its hold."

"And bows as broad as a Boston barmaid's bosom," McNiff estimated. "Terrible drag on my engine."

Captain Haylestone was reading an old copy of the *Jamaica Daily News* just before turning in when Ambrose, the spare hand of the watch, reported a ship flashing a light – trying to send a message, he thought. Haylestone came out and watched the light flashing intermittently as they passed. The vessel appeared to be stopped.

"That's morse code, ain't it, Skipper?" Ambrose commented.

"Guess so," the captain replied after an interval. He reached up and found the butt of a cigar on the shelf above the flag locker.

The lamp was still flashing astern after fifteen minutes and this gave Haylestone a sense of alarm. He never professed to read morse and sometimes regretted that he could not do so without considerable mental exertion, which generally wasn't worth it. He began to wonder if the stopped vessel was in distress. He pulled at one side of his long moustache as he leaned against the open port door gazing back. Could be in distress, he thought. Well, if he felt queasy about it he had better try his radio telephone.

He went into his cabin and irritably switched it on. He waited a minute for it to warm up and then squeezed the transmitter.

"*Maid of Jeddore . . . Maid of Jeddore.* Anyone handy using a signal lamp? What's the trouble? What's the trouble? Over."

Almost instantly a crackling voice returned.

"*Maid of Jeddore . . . Atlantic Samson* calling. Yes,

Cap. Calling you for last half hour. Something wrong with your radio? Over."

"*Atlantic Samson . . . Maid of Jeddore.* Not good. Not good. Might break down any moment. Over."

"*Maid of Jeddore* . . . this is Tug *Atlantic Samson.* Yeah, yeah. Okay. Have you seen a barge around. Over."

Tug! Barge! Haylestone did not squeeze the instrument at once. When he did he spoke slowly.

"*Atlantic Samson . . . Maid of Jeddore.* Say again. Radio bad. Over."

"*Maid of Jeddore . . . Maid of Jeddore . . . Atlantic Samson.* Have you passed a barge? Have you passed a barge . . . a barge? Over."

"*Jeddore . . . Jeddore.* Calling Tug *Atlantic Samson.* Can't get you right. Radio cracking up. Have to shut down or it'll burn up. Have to shut down. If you said large – no. My vessel's small. Out."

He jammed the transmitter onto the hook of the radio, took a few strides into the wheel-house and looked out the door again. Presently he had a deeper feeling of alarm. As he watched, the *Atlantic Samson's* lights grew obviously brighter; he could even see the light at her masthead swaying as the tug rolled in the swell. Suddenly the barge appeared in vivid brilliance. Every foot of its length was as clear as a glittering beach on a sunny day. The beam of the light which had lit it stretched back to the *Atlantic Samson.* There was no trying to hide the barge against a searchlight like that.

After a minute it swept slowly along the tow lines, as though looking for rats abandoning a doomed ship, and settled its blinding intensity on the *Maid of Jeddore.* It went out as suddenly as it had first appeared and was replaced by a raucous utterance from a loud hailer.

"That's my barge you got, Cap."

The battle joined, Haylestone felt relief. He let the sound drift away on the breeze.

"That's my barge you're towing, Cap. Lost it in the hurricane four days ago."

"Elmer," Haylestone said in a steady tone. "Go up on top of the wheel-house and take the cover off the searchlight and focus it on the tug." He told the mate to stand by the switch inside.

"That's the *Maid of Jeddore,* ain't it?" came the gutteral voice. "Cap. Do you hear me?" The pitch was an octave higher.

"Ready, Skipper," Elmer called down.

There was silence except for the muffled putt-putt of the diesel and the swish of the bow wave passing down her sides as the little freighter forged her way along beside the tug. Then the hush was broken: "Switch on, Merv."

In that instant the tug was lit like a moon. Haylestone's practiced eyes scanned her. She was big for a tug; longer perhaps than his own vessel and infinitely more powerful. A black hull with white and green upperworks and a fat raked funnel. An ocean-going tug obviously, and American built. He knew the exposed feeling her skipper would have; like standing naked in a hotel lobby.

The *Maid's* searchlight was old but of the intense carbon variety and Haylestone knew it had a limited endurance. When he felt he had displayed his opponent adequately and before the instrument gave up, he ordered it switched off.

"What the hell are you playing at," the tugboat skipper bellowed. "When are you going to give me my barge?"

Haylestone cupped his hands to his mouth and inhaled deeply.

"Don't understand you, Cap." His voice had the range of a foghorn. "You speak like you own this barge."

"That's my barge. You picked it up somewhere and I'm going to get it."

"You'll find yourself under arrest when you get into port if you attempt an act of piracy on the high seas. Where do you hail from?"

"Philadelphia. I'll take it at daylight."

Those were the last words from the *Atlantic Samson* of Philadelphia. She veered away and took up a position two miles off, steering a parallel course.

Dawn broke cold and windy. Clouds menaced the sky. The *Atlantic Samson,* outlined against the grey horizon, drew in.

"Dirty looking morning, Cap," came the voice across the now rough and noisy gap between them. "I'll put a man aboard the barge and cast off your lines when you're ready to heave them in."

"Who are you?" Haylestone roared. "What authority have you got? Come out to sea as if you owned the ocean and everything on it. I've never seen you before; and don't want to see any more of you. You're not putting a man aboard that barge and I'm not letting it go."

"If you're looking for salvage you'll regret your action, Mister," the tug skipper shouted back.

Haylestone knew he could not bluff his way into a claim of ownership. But the right of salvage and the onus of proof on the part of anyone else, he felt, put him in a commanding position. And the term 'mister' made him gag like a seasick passenger.

"I'm protecting property. You haven't shown me any evidence of ownership."

"I'm going to report your action to the State Department," was the immediate response.

"You can tell it to the President if you like . . . Mister."

Mervin Quail said afterwards that he thought at that point the tug was going to swing in and ram the *Maid.* She seemed to make a feint but instead dropped back abreast of the barge. All hands were tense. McNiff was standing outside his engine room door aft shouting down periodically to the second engineer to keep the throttle wide open. Haylestone was discharging blasphemy at the tug captain's unhearing ears, interspersed with sharp blasts on the air horn. But nothing was deterring him. It looked like an operation which Haylestone thought the navy would call "cutting out." But what defence could he put up?

The tug was now a hundred feet off the barge, pitching into the rough sea. Suddenly there was a sharp report. A puff of smoke was seen fluttering away from the tug's bridge. A thin rod shot across the barge with a line trailing behind it.

"Line-throwing gun," Quail exploded. "Spare-me-days! He's going to try to put men aboard."

Haylestone leapt to the boat deck to get a clearer view. Then he waved an arm. "Get my bear gun! My bear gun, Merv. In my cabin."

But a gun was no use without shells.

He jumped back and swung through the wheelhouse into his cabin, crashing into Elmer who had just taken the gun out of the rack. He pulled open a drawer under his bunk and scrabbled about in it.

Back on the boat deck he spotted a man in the bow with a hawser resting on the rail. The barge and tug were only fifty feet apart. Haylestone brought his gun up to his shoulder. "If he can use a gun so can I."

The report shook the rigging. The bolt rattled and another salvo rang out. Seagulls scattered.

"You got him, Hiram," shouted McNiff from the after deck. He knew the sound of that gun. "Shot away his radar and put a hole through the wheelhouse window."

The *Atlantic Samson* sheered away from the barge and the man in the bow could be seen crouching down. In five minutes she was a mile away.

The tug trailed the *Maid of Jeddore* all day. Mist developed just before dark and Haylestone, nearing home ground, knew instinctively what the weather was going to do. He swung his vessel around from her northerly course to west and rubbed his large hands when he saw the *Atlantic Samson* turn and follow. Her skipper would suspect that he had decided to head for Boston, perhaps short of fuel.

Soon after four bells in the first watch, the tug's lights were blotted out. A few minutes later a damp veil of fog enveloped the *Maid of Jeddore.* "Starboard," Haylestone ordered. The helmsman pulled his wheel over. "Steady on North." He knew the tug could not follow by radar because it had been shot away.

Around five in the morning the sea calmed down and the fog lifted. No light could be seen anywhere on the horizon.

The chief engineer was sitting on his settee rolling an after-breakfast cigarette. His body remained vertical though his well-padded buttocks moved constantly as his cabin swayed back and forth. But the movement would soon cease; they had sighted the Lurcher Light Ship, guardian of the Bay of Fundy. He was listening carefully to the radio news from his favourite Halifax station, now within range. They had been without news for more than a week, and there was a federal election coming up. Suddenly his begrimed fingers stopped twirling the cigarette paper and his whole frame stiffened as though stricken with a seizure. The radio announcer's voice was interrupted occasionally by crackling sounds but for the most part it was exceedingly clear:

"The mystery of the atomic-laden barge in the Atlantic is still unsolved," the cultured voice said. "The *Maid of Jeddore*, the little wooden boat known in the Maritimes as a double-ender, accused by the United States as having piratically seized the barge off the American coast, has not been heard from in spite of every effort by the Canadian Coast Guard and that of the United States to find her. The ocean-going tug *Atlantic Samson*, now limping into Boston, reported yesterday that the hijacker opened gunfire which holed her compass and blew away her radar. It is not known what armament the Canadian vessel possessed but the tug captain, in a radio message, surmised it was an anti-tank gun or a vintage cannon of some sort. He said that her radio was very poor. A note from Washington has already reached Ottawa concerning the seizure but its content has not been revealed. The U.S. State Department is said to be embarrassed because the disposal of atomic waste in the deeps of the Atlantic and the shipping of it through Philadelphia has never been divulged for fear of an unfavourable reaction by citizens. It is expected that the opposition here will accuse the government, in its general election campaign now being waged, of permitting merchant ships to be armed like the navy and to practice piracy on the high seas. Port authorities in Halifax say they would not permit an atomic-laden vessel to enter the harbour, nor do they believe any other port would. Word of the whereabouts and safety of the *Maid of Jeddore* is anxiously awaited. Programs on this station will be interrupted as the mystery unfolds."

Angus McNiff staggered to his feet, tobacco dropping out of his half-made cigarette, and made for the deck. He leapt up the bridge ladder like a piston and burst into the wheel-house where Haylestone was entering his minimal remarks in the log book.

"Hiram! Atomic bombs! Barge is full of atomic bombs! Got it on the radio. And they're after us. On the radio. There's hell abrewing. But they've got it all wrong. They say we practically seized . . . piratically seized the barge, and a lot more balony. We're the big news bulletin; a mystery. We got to do something."

Haylestone dropped his pencil stub. His brown eyes were wide and his moustache twitched. He suddenly made a lunge and nearly crushed McNiff against the door in his exit. He stood on the little bridge staring at the plain black barge astern rising and falling rhythmically, loaded with . . .

"Bombs did you say?" he hurled back. "Atomic bombs!"

"Why no," McNiff was breathing easier. "Come to think of it, it was atomic waste or fallout or something. It was pretty secret stuff – and of course that's why the barge has no writing on it. Washington's up in arms and Ottawa's catching it. The general election may hinge on us."

Haylestone glared at his chief engineer. "What the hell are you burbling about? Make a clear statement, Angus; a clear statement."

McNiff told the captain to come inside the wheelhouse; he was shivering too much to speak coherently. His story unfolded more or less as the radio had described it. Haylestone became quite incensed at the cannon allegation – almost to the exclusion of more pertinent matters – but he rather fancied the anti-tank gun thought. Then he came back to realities.

"I'll cast the dang thing adrift."

"Can't. The *Maid of Jeddore* was named as the party of the first part – or second part, I didn't catch which – in an international incident."

"International incident! By thunder! . . . "

He was too close in now anyway to lose the barge. He looked desolately out of the window. The coast of Nova Scotia was bathed in sunshine and shadow, the green and yellow shades of autumn sloping gently down to the foreshore. But Haylestone noticed none of these things. What he did see was a blue-hulled vessel bearing down on him – the Royal Canadian Mounted Police boats had a distinctiveness that could not be mistaken.

The vessel rounded to and her captain shouted across that he was coming aboard; would the *Maid of Jeddore* please slow down. It was the voice of Inspector Pogson, an old acquaintance of Haylestone's. The inspector and a corporal were soon climbing the short rope ladder.

Inspector Pogson was glad to see Captain Haylestone. This was a visit which he felt he had to make personally. He was interested in the barge the captain was towing. He just wanted the facts. The corporal would record them; there was no need really to caution him about what he said.

In the small cabin the two men faced one another, each handsome but each of a different cut. Captain Hiram Haylestone gave a very brief and simple account of salvaging the barge, evidently blown out to sea in the recent hurricane and a danger to navigation. He was taking it to Saint John, his next port of call.

"Did you see a tug called the *Atlantic Samson?*" Inspector Pogson asked. But Haylestone did not have a chance to answer. The mate came to report the Coast Guard alongside. With that a Canadian Coast Guard officer appeared at the door.

"Good morning, Captain Haylestone. Orders to the Coast Guard to board you as soon as sighted, Sir."

"Well," was all Haylestone felt like uttering.

"There seems to be some overlapping of authority here," Inspector Pogson remarked, eyeing the Coast Guard captain belligerently. "You'd better stay down on deck until I've discussed a few things with the captain."

But the coast guard captain was a determined type and elected to stay where he was. Haylestone was thereupon treated to an argument that became more heated as time went on, and a few things were revealed about the operation of the RCMP and about the administration of the Department of Transport of which Captain Haylestone had been previously quite unaware. Just as the policeman, in Haylestone's opinion, was getting the upper hand, the man at the wheel interrupted with a hail that would have done credit to his captain.

"Naval ships ahead, Skipper."

They stood aside as best the space would allow to let the captain out. Then they all followed.

Two destroyers were executing a splendid manoeuvre, turning inwards together under full rudder and bringing up ahead of the *Maid of Jeddore* just beyond the two ships on either side of her. They hoisted red flags simultaneously to Haylestone's disgust. "Where's the danger," he growled. Then there started a series of messages.

Captain Haylestone was ordered to repair on board the senior destroyer; a boat would be dispatched for him. This Haylestone refused to accept and it was objected to by Pogson and by the Coast Guard captain. Nevertheless a big motor boat was launched. But it drifted silently by, and was soon far astern. McNiff, standing on deck beneath the bridge to catch such conversation as came his way, rubbed his hands knowing, as he said afterwards, the navy could seldom start a motor.

A six-oared whaler came next but when the bowman failed to catch the rope thrown to him from the *Maid,* it also lost ground and no amount of strenuous rowing seemed to prevent it from dropping astern.

So the senior destroyer, apparently having no suitable conveyance, dispatched the captain of his consort to board the *Maid of Jeddore.*

In the fug of the little cabin, Canada's marine services seemed to have difficulty in establishing a rapport. Who should take command and how were the others to relinquish the task imposed upon them by their respective government departments? When the cook's lunch bell reached Haylestone's ears, he felt it was time to order drinks. So he sent for two more units of cargo and pointed out – and he had to use his voice loudly – that the sun was over the yard arm.

As far as he could gather, Ottawa had responded gracefully to Washington's demand to apprehend what the latter, in effect, described as a late model Canadian privateer, and they wanted a full explanation of the circumstances of the seizure of American property.

The rum flowed fast, and Haylestone had to remove his chart of the Western Atlantic to prevent it getting splashed and marred by the mugs. Conviviality increased and after an hour all were aglow with *bonhomie.* Then Haylestone suggested lunch.

In the mess-room they persuaded him to tell the story of the "piracy." To this he agreeably consented.

His recital evoked much mirth and he even sent the cook up for his bear gun so that he could portray more graphically how they fought it out like the *Shannon* and the *Chesapeake*.

It was three in the afternoon when they all very cordially agreed to Pogson's idea that the barge should be anchored off Partridge Island, well outside the Harbour of Saint John, and bloody well left there until the Americans wanted to pick it up; that Haylestone was to go into port and discharge his cargo, and that the Coast Guard would recommend Captain Hiram Haylestone and his brave crew for awards from the insurer of the barge, or the U.S. Government, in recognition of his fine salvage work. Pogson further suggested that the Royal Canadian Navy should make the report to Ottawa on their joint behalf. The naval officer said he would be glad to have his flotilla commander write the report – he didn't like him anyway.

Captain Haylestone, Mate Quail, and Chief Engineer McNiff stood on the little bridge of the *Maid of Jeddore,* like the conquerors of Everest, and cast their eyes about them. Fanning out with curving wakes and plumes of smoke were the ships of a great nation; services of Prevention, Protection and Defence. The trio on the bridge felt admiration for them all. And not far ahead, basking in the sunshine, lay Partridge Island, surmounted by a noble lighthouse.

# Cruising

The chief engineer puffed angrily at his bent cigarette as he sat perspiring in his accustomed seat at the end of the mess-room table. Captain Haylestone was reading from the *St. Thomas Herald,* the Virgin Islands' daily, with inflections befitting the newspaper report of the dramatic way in which his vessel had negotiated the latter part of her voyage. The mate, resting his heavy frame on the bench, held his pipe a little way from his open mouth and listened attentively.

"'It is believed to be the first time within living memory,'" Captain Haylestone read, "'that a propeller-driven ship has come into this harbour under full sail. Old timers around the wharf were thrilled when they saw the *Maid of Jeddore,* a Canadian Nova Scotiaman of 150 tons, sailing gallantly in after traversing many miles of ocean with a broken engine. Captain Hiram Haylestone, not a stranger to this port, has every reason to be flushed with pride at his superb seamanship.'"

The captain lowered the paper and, shifting the marmalade jar, laid it flat on the table to examine more closely the photograph of his little wooden vessel and the insert at the top left of her handsome master in a salt-faded cap with a tarnished gold peak above a massive bronze face. Mate Mervin Quail shifted along the bench and twisted his head around to look at the picture. The cook, who had been standing in the doorway between the galley and the mess-room, stepped inside and looked over the captain's shoulder. Only Chief Engineer Angus McNiff ignored the evidence of the great epic.

"You'll soon be flushed with more than pride, Hiram," he rumbled, "when you get to swallowing the Virgins rum. No mention there of the struggle I had, of course. The reporter didn't interview me. You gave him the dope I suppose and didn't mention the tribulations of your chief engineer."

The *Maid of Jeddore* had left Halifax with a cargo of flour for the Virgin Islands. Well south of Bermuda, in fact, just as she crossed the Tropic of Cancer, her propeller slowed down and then ceased to revolve. Angus McNiff reported a main bearing had gone and one of the bottom ends was suspect. He could not go on and he could not ship the spare at sea. There had been much argument, recrimination, castigation, and general abuse hurled between the bridge and engine room, but McNiff held on grimly, insisting that no self-respecting marine engineer would turn his propeller-shaft in a burnt out bearing.

Rolling inert in the trade wind was not a situation Hiram Haylestone enjoyed. Nor did he want to stagnate in the weeds of the Sargasso Sea. It had only fleetingly crossed his mind that he might send out a distress signal and call for a tow. Many would, but not Haylestone. Tugs cost a fortune. The one way out, he finally concluded, was to sail her.

This seemed a tall order because the Virgins were 300 miles away, and they were also the nearest land. His mainsail had been up most of the voyage. Like a fishing trawler, he used it when the wind was abaft the beam to steady her rolling.

He told the mate to bend on the jib which they had not used since last winter. He was uncertain whether they even had the foresail they had once possessed, but Mervin Quail said it was stowed away in the hold with the gaff. It was not in very good shape when they got it out but they rigged it, and in spite of the freshness of the trade wind, it did not split. With all three sails set the *Maid of Jeddore* parted the mats of seaweed and glided along at about a walking pace. Haylestone was quite jubilant about it. "Like we were back in the old schooner days, eh Merv?" he said to the mate.

They made the Island of St. Thomas in five days. There they tasted the sweet flavour of popular acclaim: and found the facilities they needed to rejuvenate the machinery.

Hiram Haylestone and Angus McNiff liked what they saw at Sam Wellington's yard on the waterfront of the Island's town of Charlotte Amalie. After half an hour with Sam Wellington, a tall handsome black, they invited him aboard to quote on repairs. This he did and the sum named for hauling the *Maid* up on his slip, withdrawing the shaft and fitting the new bearings, sounded reasonable though hard on the coffers of a simple trader.

So after the cargo was discharged, the *Maid* was taken out of the water. But the yard was slow; time dragged for Haylestone as much as it must have done for the Children of Israel in Egypt. He wanted to get away and pick up a profitable cargo without incurring the expense of prolonged idleness in this intolerably expensive outpost of American tourism. Shipowners, among them Hiram Haylestone who owned his vessel, fear idleness as much as hurricanes.

When it came to reconnecting the shaft to the engine, Sam Wellington announced that it would take longer than he had expected and the cost would go beyond his original quotation. Many other items of repair had cropped up. It appeared to Haylestone that it would take weeks to restore order below; and he might find Sam Wellington refusing to do more unless payment was forthcoming, and perhaps seizing his vessel for indebtedness. But McNiff had had the essentials done: the shaft and main bearing, and the maid was afloat again – waiting.

CRUISING

The thoroughfare along the sea front where island traders, expensive yachts, and the *Maid of Jeddore* lay was too busy for Haylestone to exercise his long legs. The enervating heat of the morning lowered him deeper into the abyss of despondency. Pressing on slowly with his hands behind his back, head bent, he almost ran into a little knot of people beside the dock. He sensed it was a collection of tourists alighting from a hotel bus. As his progress was interrupted he took shelter from the sun under a palm tree. He noticed that the group was made up of middle-aged men and women in a wide range of sports attire. They were laughing and chattering. He wished he could laugh like that. Then they all trooped aboard a schooner lying alongside. He continued his observation. After being counted apparently, the schooner cast off in a slovenly fashion and moved out into the harbour under auxiliary power.

Then he witnessed a display of raising sail which was so surprisingly unseamanlike that his mind was taken completely off himself. It made him wince several times. As he went to the dock wall to spit over it he noticed a sign reading: "Cruise the Caribbean under Sail. Charter Cruises with Captain Mike on the Schooner *Isabel.*" Beneath, in small letters he read: "Trade Wind Cruises Inc., Nat Fish."

Haylestone looked across the dancing water at the slatting sails of the schooner. Then he strode back aboard, erect, his beard jutting forward. As soon as his heavy boots struck the after deck he roared down the engine room for McNiff and sent a hand for the mate.

"See that?" Haylestone barked, pointing down the harbour. "Schooner. Passengers. There's money there." He faced his subordinates. "We're going into the cruising business."

Angus McNiff staggered and sank back against the after hatch, his pants, showing strain and toil in the dark wrinkles between crotch and knee, drooped more than usual.

"What in Heaven's name!" he muttered.

"Cruising, Angus. If that halfarsed schooner can do it, so can I. It's just a matter of fitting this vessel out a bit and getting the tourists aboard."

McNiff seldom collapsed but he was near it now. But Merv Quail stood stolidly, his broad suspenders straining like hawsers over his portly figure, his lips moving occasionally on his pipe stem as though repeating to himself some of his captain's words.

McNiff came back to life. "Cruising, Hiram! Cruising! You know I can't work my engine. You can't leave the dock the way we are."

"Now Angus, just listen; and you too, Merv. Here's the scheme." Haylestone pulled out a damp White Owl from his shirt pocket and with difficulty lit it. "All I want you to do, Angus, is to be able to turn your engine slowly for no more than twenty minutes. We'll sail her, by damn, after that!"

"Can't turn engine at all," McNiff spluttered.

"Yes you can."

"With a scored cylinder? Cooling system out . . . oil lines gummed up."

"Well get them ungummed. I'll need no more than twenty minutes at slow speed. That won't hurt a scored cylinder."

Having concluded the argument for the main engine, Haylestone turned to Quail.

"Get her tidied up, Merv. Scrub down the decks and wash the rails and paintwork. Can't have passengers getting themselves messed up. And that reminds me Angus: keep the soot in the box and don't let it come out of the funnel. Passengers with white yachting caps don't like soot." He hesitated. "Where'll we stow the liquor? They always have to have plenty of hooch aboard. That's where much of the profit is – I guess."

Merv Quail seemed to have absorbed quite a lot of what had been said. "In the hold. It's the coolest place."

"Too much going up and down. Have to be handier than that."

"Ruddy optimistic," McNiff interjected.

Haylestone recognized that the mate was with him, anyway. He said that was all for the moment, he was going ashore to see his agent and contact the hotels – and get a licence for the carriage of passengers.

At 9.30 a.m. two mornings later, Captain Hiram Haylestone on the bridge rang "slow ahead." The *Maid of Jeddore* moved forward – and soot shot out of the funnel.

"Jib," Haylestone shouted down to the mate. Then he ordered the foresail hoisted. He thought he detected the refrain of a chanty mingling with the rattle of the parrals against the mast. When the mainsail had gone up smartly and all sail trimmed to the breeze, he rang the telegraph to 'stop.' "Fifteen minutes," he muttered to himself. "That shouldn't disturb old Angus."

Glancing back he saw the white bus leaving his vacant berth. Below him on the fore deck were his passengers: *his* passengers, some standing entranced by the green hills of St. Thomas; some reclining in new, colourful deck chairs. There were twelve of them; just right for two sittings in the mess-room, with Haylestone attending both so that he could regale them with yarns – the PR side of the business. He hummed a tune several times, then captured the words: "Cruising down the river on a Sunday afternoon."

It had been a hectic two days selling the cruise to travel agents, hotels, and the local tourist bureau. Haylestone had no fancy white uniform like the great liner officers or the swashbuckling rig of the schooner men; he had to sweat it out in his old brass-buttoned blue reefer jacket and trousers constructed to resist the cold blasts of the sub-Arctic. But it made him an even more imposing figure; unique.

Not the least of his trials had been the urging of

McNiff to do his duty as he, the captain, saw it. Yet almost to the last minute, while stealthily connecting his diesel, McNiff fought against the violation of engineering principles. Had Haylestone known McNiff's true intent he would not have cut him in on five per cent of the take.

He appointed Elmer barman and conducted a seminar in the dispensing of liquor.

It was a day trip. As he had noticed on the schooner, the passengers were mostly early middle-aged tourists, apparently willing to pay twenty dollars each, which included a fish hash noon dinner, plus liquor charges.

As the *Maid of Jeddore* cleared Flamingo Point and bore away to the Capella Islands, the booms creaked and the rigging sang sweetly. The sun dappled the blue sea to leeward where the flying fish played, and a low hiss came from the bow wave. Haylestone was happy; everyone was happy. Even McNiff seemed keen.

It was probably the first time in her many years on the high seas that a skirt had fluttered on the fore deck. Quite a charming sight, Haylestone thought. By mid-afternoon some couples had climbed the ladder to the boat deck, a region Haylestone had always heard was morally hazardous in passenger ships; but liners were probably not soot-ridden.

At sunset the *Maid* glided into the harbour before the wind fell away. She may have looked an oddity; a wooden motor vessel under heavy squat sails; nothing like the tall sleek yachts moored off Charlotte Amalie's waterfront. Yet her passengers thought she was sturdily elegant. But they couldn't see themselves as others saw them. The trip was a signal success. The only men it had been really hard on were the cook and Elmer, and they had been rewarded by some unaccustomed gratuities. The next day it was a case of turning customers away.

After a week Haylestone had a visit from Trade Wind Cruises Inc. in the person of Mr. Nat Fish who said that his business was suffering from unfair competition. Haylestone said that with a lug like Captain Mike, who might as well be asleep ten fathoms down as on deck, how could he expect to withstand fair, not unfair, competition. But Mr. Nat Fish made it evident that he was an influence ashore and could stifle Haylestone's business at its source. He had no objection to longer cruises; he was not in the market for more than day trips.

So Haylestone announced they would do three-day cruises. Since he could not carry as many people, his rates would be much higher – and his bar receipts greater. All he had to do was to install an awning over the fore deck, which was needed anyway, and sling hammocks beneath it to form a sort of open-air dormitory. He told McNiff he would have to put a shower or tub in the heads. There was plenty of room; it just meant removing the coils of rope that shared the place with the toilet.

Protests about plumbing difficulties were stamped out, and in the two days that it took to rig the vessel for overnight passenger travel Haylestone bought a second-hand refrigerator to make ice, notified the hotels of his extended cruises and had a colourful sign erected on the dock advertising, "Vagabond Cruises on the *Maid of Jeddore.* Captain Hiram Haylestone, Master."

Two vagabond cruises a week were made and they were pleasant, moving slowly along under tropic skies in zephyrs that never failed. They were a success too. A new foresail had been acquired and bent on in case the old one blew away. Sam Wellington had been paid up to date, and there was almost enough in hand now to finish the engine repairs. And McNiff was making money with his five per cent.

Back once more in St. Thomas, one of the travel agents came to Haylestone. Could a group charter the boat for a week's cruise? The visitors wanted to see some of the Leeward Islands. They seemed to be educationalists from Pittsburgh. Haylestone agreed for a good figure and took aboard a larger quantity of stores.

They sailed from Charlotte Amalie in warm sunshine with here and there a soft white cloud, like a puff of steam, floating aloft. Though this climatic loveliness persisted, life for the crew of the *Maid of Jeddore* for the first time became rough and jolty.

To start with the wind was east by north and, as they dropped the green hills of the Virgins and met the breeze of the deeper sea, they could not sail close enough to make good a course to the Leeward Islands. Then, when Elmer came for orders from the bar, none of the passengers wanted a drink. All eight were women.

There was barely room for Haylestone at the messroom table. Looking round, he thought he had never seen such hard-visaged spinsters since he had left school. They were not ill groomed. They were not wearing shorts. He felt that was just as well. They were modestly colourful.

A thin, upright person at the end of the table, with grey hair screwed back, offered the information that Miss Robinson was not present. "She's seasick," she stated, as though her confrere had broken her leg through not looking where she was going. "She wanted us to put up her hammock but we said no, she'd be much better on her feet."

A woman with gold-rimmed glasses, who had evidently been keeping her mouth clear for speech while Miss Wynce had been making her remarks, said she thought dining saloons were always downstairs in passenger boats. "When I travelled to Europe on the *United States* some years ago, we went way down in an elevator."

"No elevators aboard here, Ma'am," Haylestone snorted. "Nor stairs; they're ladders."

Miss Wynce had lifted her plate and was moving it

from side to side as though looking for worms beneath a flat stone. "Is there a shortage of cutlery, Captain? It seems I've only been provided with three pieces." She put her plate down and looked at Haylestone with head tilted back. "I consider the travel agent misled us. He said your boat had all the facilities necessary for a voyage. I agreed, on behalf of us girls, that we might sleep on deck in hammocks because I felt that was something we could do. But the bathroom! There's no hot-water faucet in the basin. And it looks as if the shower, a crude arrangement, is the same. I may have more to say about the bathroom," she added.

"What do you want hot water for in the tropics?" Haylestone snapped.

"The captain may be right, dear." It was the person on his right who spoke. While she appeared to come to his rescue, Haylestone was struck by her fat faulty smile; her eyes were malevolent in spite of her words. Something like a small white handkerchief was pinned to her up-swept hair which made her head look like a cactus in flower. "On a voyage like this there's no need to wash."

"Oh, I can't agree with you there, Mildred," said Miss Wynce in a rather shocked voice. But Mildred was wading into her rapidly emptying plate. Haylestone had wondered how she had wedged herself in behind the mess table; and how she could see her food below her bosom.

"Why haven't you got a fan in here?" she asked suddenly, collapsing back and mopping her mulberry face.

"No real need," Haylestone said.

"Oh, yes there is. It's stifling . . . Well, why haven't you?"

"I told you, Miss . . . "

"Miss Scantelbury," she informed him. "And I won't accept 'no need' for an answer."

For once Haylestone held his peace, though it was difficult. He had never seen anything quite like Miss

Mildred Scantelbury – in size, appearance, or character.

One of the ladies rose unsteadily to her feet. Miss Scantelbury wanted to know if she was going to be seasick too. She chuckled mirthlessly. "It's all mental, you know. Well, go and feed the fishes if you want."

"Please, Mildred." Even Miss Wynce had her moments of compassion.

For the first time in his life, the captain barked a shin on the high step of the galley door as he came out on deck. He had left his pie and coffee untouched.

Complaints poured in all afternoon and periodically on the next day. Almost everything was touched on. There was no lounge, no library. Where were the card tables and chairs? Where were the salads? Why weren't they sighting the Lesser Antilles?

In the heat of the third afternoon, as the *Maid of Jeddore* bore up to windward as closely as she could sail, Haylestone was suddenly awakened by a penetrating shriek. Leaping out of his deck chair on the open bridge, he looked down on the awning over the fore deck. He heard moans and female voices and little cries. Someone was coming up the ladder. It was Miss Wynce.

"Captain! Come at once! It's Miss Scantelbury. She's collapsed."

She had indeed. Within a short while the captain had to pronounce her dead. Heart, obviously.

Haylestone called the hands and they laid her out on the fore hatch, her enormous bulk suitably chocked off with dunnage against the movement as the vessel wore around to the starboard tack; and after the ladies had paid their tearless tributes and duly spoken of their regret about the lack of flowers, she was taken aft. They placed her in one of the hammocks which, on more cheerfully boisterous voyages, had been reserved for passengers who had collapsed but not succumbed.

The sun was still hot in the sky when Miss Wynce

came aft and questioned Captain Haylestone about his plans.

"Very sad. Poor Miss Scantelbury," she started appropriately. "But she was too heavy. You'll be back in St. Thomas tomorrow of course."

"No. It'll be three days before we're back."

"Three days! Oh no, Captain. We've got to be back tomorrow."

"How?" Haylestone drawled.

"You ought to know."

"We're off Martinique. Three days journey to the Virgins."

"But we must get the late Miss Scantelbury back to Pittsburgh as quickly as possible."

"The corpse won't get to Pittsburgh, Ma'am."

Miss Wynce felt for the rail as though she were about to seize a belaying pin. "Oh? . . . And where will she reach, pray?"

"Davie Jones's locker, Ma'am. That is, we shall bury the corpse at sea tomorrow morning."

"At sea! Bury the remains of the late Mildred Scantelbury at sea! But that's not right. Can't you go into Martinique or some island where she can have a decent funeral if we can't get her to Pittsburgh?"

"Nothing indecent in a funeral at sea. I can't get into Martinique or any other island. They all lie to windward."

"What's that got to do with it?"

"This vessel doesn't beat to windward well; and the wind is too far to the east. I'm heading back to the Virgins."

"I wish we'd never come on your wretched boat. Why can't we keep her till we reach the Virgin Islands?"

Haylestone glanced towards the hammock and up at the sun. "We're in the tropics, Ma'am," was all Haylestone cared to say.

Towards four o'clock the next morning, the mate took two hands aft. With commendable reverence they wound the corpse in canvas with a heavy weight, which they obtained from McNiff, at the foot. "Pretty buoyant things, corpses, when not loaded," Quail told his men. Quail did the sewing under lights which threw deep, moving shadows as they swung from the rigging. He sent Ed and Ambrose down the hold to find some eight-foot boards with instructions to make a skid. They did their sawing down below and when they came up they put it together with muffled hammers. The boat moved through the ruffled sea almost silently.

When Quail had put his needle through the last bit of tough sail cloth and knotted the twine they went forward, satisfied that everything was in readiness for the funeral at ten o'clock. But Haylestone wanted to make sure; he had seen the best laid preparations slip up for want of practice. They proceeded aft again, headed by the captain.

Haylestone first examined the skid. It was long, about three feet wide, and had low sides. Ambrose and Ed lifted it up and placed the outer end on the bulwark rail to show the captain how it balanced. They rested the inboard end on the hatch so that it lay horizontally across the deck. Haylestone walked around it and leaned on it to see if it was strong enough, then squinted along it as though he were taking a sextant angle. He removed his cap and hung it on the pump handle by the door of the heads. The others were bare-headed.

An examination of the work Merv had done assured him that the corpse was well parcelled up with as neat stitching as he could wish to see. It seemed very bulky though. He tried lifting one end; he liked its rigidity.

"You'd better try it for fit," he told Quail. "Hoist it aboard."

"Lay hold, boys," Merv Quail directed as he reached down. "One – two – three, heave-ho."

In the pinkish grey light of coming day muscles stood out on bare arms.

Merv Quail surveyed the result closely. "Push the corpse more this way. . . . Okay, that's square."

"Fits well," Ed pronounced, looking along the edges of his skid.

"Ought to," Quail answered slowly, "I gave you the measure of it."

Haylestone now seriously questioned whether the skid would hinge on the rail properly with such a weight. "It might bend too much, or snap. Wouldn't do for something like that to happen in front of the passengers, especially that Wynce woman. Try it, Merv. Lift it up a piece."

Merv Quail regarded the skid and its burden silently; then told Ed and Ambrose to man the inner end. "Angus. You and I'll hold the corpse here." McNiff, an early riser when unemployed, had just come on deck.

He took as firm a grip as the hard canvas would allow and looked up at the men at the head of the skid. "Hoist away, handsomely."

It was indeed a heavy lift, but Haylestone noted that the outboard end was hinging on the rail, though it squeaked like an old door. He stood back a little to review the affects of load.

Suddenly the corpse moved.

McNiff shouted, "Astern!" Merv Quail yelled, "Avast!" Then it slid past the mate and chief engineer, gathering momentum.

Haylestone bellowed, "Hold it," and leaped forward with outstretched arms. He fetched up against an unoccupied skid. McNiff, in his effort to hold the moving object, was thrown off balance and fell to the deck.

As the skid came down with a bang on the hatch, Quail saw the remains of the late Miss Scantelbury sail through the air and hit the water end-on – McNiff's machinery end – and disappear with no more splash than would have been made by a pelican diving for a fish.

Hiram Haylestone flung his arms to heaven and shouted, "Good God!"

Ed and Ambrose were silenced as though they had been condemned to death. Merv Quail and McNiff, now on his feet, were leaning over the rail gazing towards the pale green wake, perhaps hoping that it would remain afloat. But Angus McNiff knew better; he was familiar with the specific gravity of his weight.

"Spare-me-days," muttered Quail.

"What the hell are you looking astern for?" Haylestone roared. "It's a hundred fathoms below now." He stamped back across the deck.

Disturbed as McNiff was, he was quick to grasp the situation. He took the captain's battered cap off the pump handle and handed it to him. He told him to pipe down. "Stop bellowing like a bull, Hiram. You'll have that lot for'ard pouring aft here to see who's murdering who."

Haylestone glanced quickly up both sides of the deck. The clarity of view suddenly made him realize that the tropical sunrise was nearly on them. The stars had disappeared and the mainmast rose clear towards the limpid sky. He glanced back at the skid. It was empty all right – clean, stark empty. He wiped the sweat from his forehead.

"What are we going to do now?" he breathed in a hoarse whisper, glancing up the deck again. "They'll be on us like a bunch of cormorants when they find out. They expect a funeral and I've got no corpse."

Captain Haylestone felt as if he had reached the dead water at the end of an ebb tide. A great red ball appeared over the horizon. The faint swish of the water past the vessel's side became unusually audible.

Then, suddenly, he felt the tide begin to flood. With less warning than the equatorial sunrise, the image came.

"Get another body, Merv." The command was sharp.

Quail looked at the captain.

"Merv. Another corpse."
"Another what?"
"Corpse . . . C O R P S. Thing you just lost."
"Corpse? Where from?"
"Make one."

McNiff exploded. "That's it. Of course. Can't you see, Merv? A dummy . . . dummy, Merv. Hiram's saying cook up another corpse."

Like the orb on the horizon, brilliance flooded into Quail's round face.

"Corpse . . . corpse . . . same as we lost. I got it! Dummy. Aye, aye. I got it, Hiram."

Beneath the half-masted ensign, in the deep shadow of the mainsail, two men stood at the head of the burial skid. It was ten o'clock. The American flag shrouded its burden. On one side stood Captain Hiram Haylestone, hot in his brass-buttoned jacket; on the other Mate Mervin Quail, the same in a blue sweater. The chief engineer was standing at attention, as best he knew how, at his engine room door. The passengers were assembled along the starboard side.

The captain waved his arm, the cook on the boat deck passed the word and the man at the wheel put the helm down. The vessel swung into the wind and stopped like a hovering bird.

With bared head Captain Haylestone read from The Shipmaster's Medical Guide, a volume containing, as a postscript to the identity and treatment of every foreign disease, prayers for the burial of the dead at sea. At the appropriate words about committing the body to the deep the mate murmured, "Up" and the skid was raised. A single splash recorded the commitment. No one looked over the side, but in a few moments the passengers could see little ripples going out in half circles from the boat.

As Haylestone closed his Medical Guide the Canadian ensign moved slowly up and fluttered once more at the truck, and the *Maid of Jeddore* squared away on the starboard tack.

One of the ladies in a hushed voice called, "Captain." Haylestone walked bravely across the deck.

"It was beautiful," said Miss Wynce. "We have some photos to take back to Pittsburgh."

The passengers disembarked under the hot afternoon sun and climbed into the white hotel bus. Haylestone glowered at its rear end as it moved off. "I hate women!" he snarled.

McNiff stood on the fore deck beside him, his hands holding a newly rolled cigarette before his mouth like a harmonica player about to start on a low note. "But passengers sure pay, Hiram . . . We'll see Sam Wellington tomorrow?"

"Tomorrow, first thing, Angus. Time we were back in the cargo trade again."

McNiff ran the cigarette paper over his tongue and sank back against the bulwark.

# The Foul Trophy

Angus McNiff stood outside the wheel-house with Captain Haylestone as the *Maid of Jeddore* cleared Boston Harbour with package freight for Halifax. McNiff stared up at the blue afternoon sky as though he could see a couple of pressure gauges registering the cooler air over the ocean outside. Hiram Haylestone looked down at the chief.

"No use you looking up there, Angus. An engineer can't foretell the weather. Not like a navigator."

McNiff's gaze followed the downward flight of a seagull and came to rest on the black-bearded face of the captain a foot above him. Mr. McNiff's down-hanging eyebrows looked as though they must hinder his vision but, like a Skye Terrier, he could see through them. "It's going to be cooler," he predicted stolidly.

"Anybody'd know that. Bound to be cooler out at sea than in the stifling city back there in July. Give me Halifax any day of the week."

"I thought you said you wanted to fetch Halifax on a particular day of the week – Thursday, in fact. I didn't seem to hear you say any day, Hiram. Thursday, 6 a.m., was the time you were talking around."

The chief was shaking out some strands of tobacco from a round tin with his oil-blackened thumb and forefinger. Over the cigarette paper that fluttered from his lower lip he added, "And what you mean is, cooler than in that stinking tavern on Dock Street."

"Now lookit, Angus . . . "

"Lookit, nothing! You're responsible for this predicament. Like I told you in the mess-room at breakfast, you're going to get your vessel racked out – that is," he slowed down his speech, "if I do push my engine."

"Belay it, Angus!" The captain's voice could have been heard three ship's lengths away. The chief put the rolled cigarette in his mouth, bent a little and lit it against a big flame. He dropped the worn brass lighter back into the pocket of his stained pants which hung like chewed string from a belt that encircled the lower part of his drum-like belly.

"You get down to the bowels of the vessel," Haylestone shouted, his voice diminishing in strength only slightly, "and get that engine turning like it's never turned before. It's to be Thursday, 6 a.m., and not a moment later."

"So you said," McNiff replied, turning round reflectively and putting a dull-black, oil-soaked shoe on the top step of the ladder leading down to the main deck. "And supposing I do sweat up my engine." He let his words hover for a moment. "Supposing I do push my diesel for you, which you don't deserve, you dang well see you cut the corners and justify your perpetual blather about fancy navigating."

Then the chief engineer of the *Maid of Jeddore* took another step down the ladder and gradually disappeared.

The question of whether he deserved it became paramount once again in Haylestone's mind. Last night in the Ship Tavern, Captain Ezekiel Klogg had taunted him beyond what the heat would allow. Haylestone knew himself to be the better navigator – a term Klogg translated to "ordinary getting round the coast" – and he still maintained, at the eighth glass of Puerto Rico rum, in an even louder voice than earlier, that he could beat any coasting skipper at navigating, and probably any deep-sea master when inside the Grand Banks.

While the doubting Captain Klogg sat scrutinizing the bar floor the bellowing ceased for a moment. Why shouldn't he put Klogg in his proper perspective, the perspective of the damned old Clam Harbour skipper he was?

"Zeke," he said, quieter, holding his glass in one hand and a White Owl stump in the other. "Zeke Klogg. I'll bet you I'll be alongside the wharf in Halifax before you and your *Ethel B*, in spite of the start you'll have on me tomorrow. I'll round the Sambro Ledges before you've even seen them too. And it'll be done by superior 'getting round the coast.'"

Klogg asked his old rival to repeat the first part of what he had said. Haylestone, in a stentorian voice, made it clear that he was prepared to bet that he'd be in Halifax first, even though the *Ethel B* was a newer vessel than his own. "I'll stake what you want."

Captain Klogg, a greying little man, looking smaller than usual across the table from Haylestone, levelled his eyes through the window of the Ship as though he were searching for Chebucto Head light. Haylestone took a long draught and waited.

"Anchor," Klogg announced at last. "Bet your anchor."

Haylestone's knees sagged wider apart as he slowly assumed a crouch in his creaky chair.

"I don't want your miserable little anchor," he shouted. The street noises harmonized with his voice so that he did not disturb the other inmates particularly.

Perhaps Klogg had known that. He replied quietly, "But I could do with yours. I could do with heavier bower anchors. But one will do in the meantime."

"Well, you won't get it because you won't win. And, as I said, I don't want your miserable mud hook, so I'll take a five-gallon keg of Schreecher's –

not this insipid Puerto Rican stuff." He scowled at his glass.

There was some argument about that, Zeke Klogg trying to whittle it down to two gallons but, after the intervention of the proprietor of the Ship, the bets were taken and witnessed: Klogg's five gallons of rum to one of Haylestone's large anchors.

So, after an hour, during which Captain Hiram Haylestone several times verbally navigated Captain Ezekiel Klogg's vessel round Egg Island and into Clam Harbour, Klogg's native village, they both returned to their respective coasters in high anticipation of a race worthy of the *Bluenose.*

The *Maid of Jeddore* was trembling as she headed towards Cape Sable, her bow sliced the smooth sea, curling it splashing up the wooden stem and sending the humpy waves rolling out from her sides.

"I'm getting all I can out of her, I tell you," McNiff was saying to the captain. "Look at them shrouds up there, shivering like a trawl with a fifty pound cod on it. That's speed."

But Haylestone was leaning over the side.

"Ten Knots," he announced. "That's all."

"Ten!" McNiff poked his head over the bulwark rail and looked down at the bubbling water slipping by. "Ten and a half."

"That's no ten and a half! And you wouldn't know if it was or it wasn't by looking at the water."

McNiff eyed the captain. "I go by the revs. It's ten and a half."

"So it better be. You know the *Ethel B* had nearly forty blasted miles start on us leaving Boston. She's near a ten-knot boat – except when Zeke misses a tide." Haylestone gripped his cigar more firmly between his bicuspids. "And you can bet Zeke is doing more than that. So you should be driving us along at darn near eleven. No less, Angus."

McNiff glared through his eyebrows. Then he relaxed and leaned back on the bulwark.

"Maybe I'll give up this coasting and go back to them deep-water ships again," he mused, unexpectedly wistful. "It was a good life on that cable ship, a good life. Out in mid-Atlantic and down the West Indies. You could save money there. And you were respected, too."

"Now, Angus," Haylestone put in soothingly, "you don't want to be thinking that way. We've been running the *Maid* together for all these years. All I want this trip is that extra half knot or so I know you can pull out of your engine."

"You were respected in deep-water ships," McNiff murmured on in a far-away voice, "for your technical knowledge and ability. And were believed when you said how you were operating your engines."

He looked towards the shores of Maine where the sun was setting and the last thin blue line of land was dipping out of sight. The pale sky flecked with small clouds had turned pink, giving a touch of warmth to the cool Atlantic air.

Haylestone spread out his massive hands. "You want to share that keg of Schreecher's with me, don't you, Angus?" The captain of the *Maid of Jeddore* believed himself to be a reasonable man.

"Ten and a half," said McNiff.

But the next day they encountered a strong head wind and had to reduce speed to prevent the vessel hitting the steep curling sea too hard in her laden condition. Haylestone was surprised to see McNiff in the middle of the morning ease himself into the wheel-house against the pressure of the wind on the door.

"Seen her yet, Hiram?"

Haylestone, who had taken the wheel himself when he had sent the helmsman down to do a job on deck, noticed that the chief had caught a load of spray on his way up. He was soaked down one side but he did not seem to care, and his hair, thinned by the effects of years of super-heated steam, was slicked down like the pelt of a wet otter.

"Who?" Haylestone asked.

"*Ethel B,* of course. Where is she?"

"Where?" This spoke well for Angus, Haylestone thought pleasantly. "I know where she is."

"Well, where? That's what I come up here to find out."

"You won't see her yet, Angus, even though Zeke's had to ease down like us. You'll see her before dark this evening."

Haylestone smiled as McNiff went below without further remark and the little ship pitched in a cork-screw fashion over another wave.

In the early afternoon Cape Sable was sighted dead ahead. Haylestone went down to the engine room door.

"Hi! Angus. Come aloft. Want to show you something."

"Is it Klogg?"

"Of course not. Not yet. Cape Sable. Hit it square on the nose. That's navigating. Come and look."

"Can't. Got to give attention down here. Don't you hear it beating up all hell. I tell you, I'm running her faster than I should and I've got to keep the bearings from seizing up."

"Okay, then, keep her going, boy."

The *Maid of Jeddore* went close into Cape Sable and inside Brazil Rock, escaping the rough sea and picking up the surging tide running out of the Bay of Fundy. They were off Little Hope Island when Haylestone sighted a small vessel broad on the star-board bow. But in the twilight he could not be at all sure who she was. She might even have been a trawler.

At two in the morning the captain was awakened by the mate's voice. "Fog's setting in, Hiram."

With giant-like noises Haylestone stumbled out through the wheel-house and onto the tiny bridge structure, rubbing his eyes. He soon saw and felt the damp, grey pall that had settled down all round. The wind had died out and the sound of the water falling away from the bow as the *Maid of Jeddore* hurried on was more audible than usual. Sure it was foggy. But he could find his way whether it was thick as a hedge or clear.

"Where are we now, Merv?" he asked the mate. He shivered: it was different from the Boston heat.

"Pretty near up to Pennant Point. Should hear the whistle buoy soon." Quail knew these waters; he came from Ketch Harbour.

Haylestone looked at the wheel-house clock and then at the compass in front of the helmsman. "We'll be up to the fairway buoy by four. The fog'll be thinner there at the harbour entrance and we'll just slide in nice and quiet as the daylight's coming in. And we'll be through breakfast before Zeke pulls in. He's scared of fog."

Mervin Quail drew on his pipe and said, "Maybe," and went on leaning out the window.

They heard the whistle of Pennant Point buoy, a mechanical, windy whistle that finished its doleful note with a jerk. But it was a friendly sound. Haylestone set a course to pass close to the South West Breakers off Sambro Island.

"Old Klogg'll be steering out into mid-Atlantic in eighty fathoms of water now," he remarked. "He doesn't like hugging the coast when it's thick. He's cautious. He shouldn't bet."

The *Maid of Jeddore* was off Chebucto Head at four, having negotiated the Ledges nicely. They could hear the fog horn high up the cliff. Then they heard the faint whistle of the fairway buoy penetrating the fog and Haylestone crept slowly up towards the sound.

But it was still as thick as ever. In fact, he had difficulty in even sighting the big red buoy in spite of its whistle. When he did come on it suddenly, he passed so close alongside it that, as it rocked towards the vessel, the lantern at the top of the tall cage leaned inboard over the bulwark. Luckily it did not tangle with the rigging. There was no sliding into harbour at dawn with a thinning fog.

"We'll have to anchor, blast it!" Haylestone announced. "Starboard a bit, Ed," he said to the man at the wheel. "Steer nor'-nor'-east. We'll put the hook down inside Thrumcap Shoal, Merv."

They caught the clink of the bell on the buoy marking the shoal, worked in a bit and dropped the anchor in five fathoms of water. Then Ed went down to the galley to brew coffee.

As the shroud of foggy darkness began to turn grey with the coming of dawn, Haylestone stood in the wheel-house with Quail and Ed. The port door was open. They alternately looked out at the weather and at the clock on the bulkhead behind the wheel.

Mervin Quail's heavy squat figure became clearly silhouetted. "Wants our anchor," he reflected. "That right, Hiram? Zeke's shrewd. Wouldn't like to wonder what he's doing now."

In the last half hour Haylestone had thought a lot about what Klogg would do. "Zeke may stand off outside . . . and then again he mightn't. He could work himself in close to Portuguese Cove across from here and hang around there."

"But he ain't a man to do that in fog," Quail observed in his husky voice."

"Might." Haylestone put his mug down on the window ledge. "Maybe I've overestimated his cautiousness."

"You haven't done that exactly, Hiram. It's his figuring."

"You mean calculating."

"Figuring," the mate insisted.

"Same thing."

"Okay then, calculating. He'll be figuring it out right now."

"Where?" Haylestone asked.

"Well, spare-me-days, Hiram, I don't know."

Ed suddenly went out. "Ain't it clearing a bit?"

Haylestone stepped outside. The sun was not quite up yet but it was clearer. Quail examined the other side.

"Aye, it's lifting all right, Hiram," he shouted across the bridge. "Conical buoy on the starboard bow a good mile off."

"That right? Okay, then. Jump down and get the anchor in quick, Merv. Looks like we could slip in now."

Haylestone watched Quail start the windlass motor and saw Elmer, the other hand of the watch, turn the water on the hose to wash the mud off the chain before it came up the hawse-pipe. The heavy links began to grind and clank as they came over the windlass.

"Heave the hook right home, Merv," the captain shouted. Then he became aware of the windlass motor slowing down. "Come on," he called. "Give her the gun, Merv. A lot may depend on speed now."

But the wretched motor suddenly coughed and stopped.

Quail glanced at it and then stepped to the bulwark and looked over.

"What's the matter," Haylestone called.

After a full minute, during which Haylestone tried several phrases to attract the mate's attention, Quail looked back at the bridge.

"Give her a touch ahead, Hiram. Chain's leading straight down but the anchor must be pretty tight into the mud."

The telegraph jangled in the wheel-house. Quail paid out the chain a bit, and then swung the flywheel of the windlass motor. He got it going fast but in a moment it sputtered out again.

Haylestone threw his fists above his head. "What's wrong with the benighted thing? What's the matter with the engine? Where's Angus? Get Angus up." McNiff got it from the wheel-house voice pipe.

The chief engineer appeared on the fore deck in his usual rig. He would not remain warm for long. Haylestone saw him put the windlass motor in neutral after a volley of opprobrious epithets and start it. He ran it for a long time making a lot of noise.

Haylestone now heard the motor pulling hard and over the straining sound he could hear the slow clank of the chain as link by link came labouring over the windlass. He could not stand it any longer. He jumped down on deck and strode towards the forecastle, black head thrust forward and the thick soles of his boots striking the deck like a hammer. He came to a halt where McNiff squatted over the engine and drew the morning air in through his nose before making himself heard over the noise.

"Now, don't let the bloody thing stop, Angus. Keep it going. If you . . . "

But a wild yell from Quail made McNiff throw the clutch out.

Haylestone jumped to the bow. Elmer dropped the hose which swung round like a snake and threw a forceful jet of sea water at McNiff as he straightened up. His cry and the words which followed went unnoticed. Elmer had joined the others at the bulwark.

McNiff kicked the hose and then glanced over the bow too.

"It's an old rope," Haylestone was saying to Quail. It was looped over the flukes of the anchor which hung dripping just above the water. It seemed to stretch out quite tightly. They were all gazing at it.

The captain broke the silence. "Must be a rope fast to something. Five-inch rope, I'd say."

"Looks to me like it's a wire hawser coated with mud," Quail said.

"No. It's a manilla rope," Haylestone contradicted. "Elmer. Get an axe."

McNiff had not bothered with more than a glance. He was back stamping his feet and squeezing out his soaking pants.

The waiting was hard on the captain. He looked searchingly over the sun-flecked wavelets towards Chebucto Head.

When Elmer returned with a long-handled axe he swung himself over the bulwark and went down the chain and found a footing on the anchor.

"Now, hit the rope just abaft the fluke, Elmer," Haylestone explained. "If you give it a good clout it ought to part with one blow. But mind your feet as it goes clear. There's quite a strain on it."

Elmer swung like an executioner and the axe blade bit. But the expected did not happen. There had been a metallic clink, yet strangely, Elmer had to work the handle to release the blade. He looked up at the captain.

"Hit it again," Haylestone ordered, with some curiosity in his voice. But his instructions were suddenly interrupted by McNiff who had come to look over again.

"Belay it, Hiram! Belay it! That ain't a rope. Elmer," he shouted down, though Elmer was just beneath him. "Avast there! Hold hard!"

Elmer lowered his axe and looked up inquiringly.

The captain swung round on McNiff. "What is it then if it isn't a rope?"

The engineer, holding the rail with his hand and pivoting away from the bulwark on his wet feet, rather like a top, faced the captain. "It's a cable! Telephone cable! And what's more it's the Atlantic telephone cable."

"Spare-me-days!" exclaimed Quail.

"Cable? Atlantic telephone cable . . . ?" Haylestone gazed down at the horrible thing to which his vessel had become immovably secured. "Cripes! Drop that axe, Elmer. No. Heave it up here." He pushed his cap to the back of his head; he was sweating.

"Feel it, Elmer," he directed the seaman on the anchor. "What d'you make of it? Rubber? Cast iron or something?"

Elmer dug at it with his thumb and ran his hand

over it. "It's hard and it ain't got the lay of a rope." He kicked it and it seemed to hurt his toe.

"Yes." McNiff spoke deliberately. "I seen the one similar many a time on that cable ship, way out at sea as well as on the coast here. In my time it was a telegraph cable. New telephone cable's the same. You better not axe that through, Hiram."

"Atlantic Cable!" Haylestone muttered. "By damn! If we cut that!"

"You've made a wedge in it already."

"It'll surely be too heavy to sling off," Haylestone speculated. "We'll drop the anchor and see if it jumps off when it hits the bottom."

"Aye, maybe it will," Quail agreed.

"All right then. Let her go."

McNiff unscrewed the brake of the windlass and the chain ran out with a roar. Haylestone was looking down at the water. He wished he had some device which would tell him what had taken place.

"Heave away again," he ordered.

The engine raced, then slowed as the clutch went home and the chain began to come in again. It slowed down still more as the weight of the anchor came on the chain.

"Still there, Cap'n," McNiff shouted over the noise of the windlass. "You'll be lucky if I can get her up."

Haylestone's temper rose a few more notches at McNiff's unfriendly use of his professional title. The anchor broke surface.

"Damn my buttons! It didn't do it . . . Let her go again."

Down went the anchor. The third time McNiff coaxed the engine the answer was obvious. The anchor appeared at the surface with the cable still laid neatly over it, like a cat's cradle over a child's hand.

Haylestone felt exhausted. McNiff screwed up the brake and came to the rail. Quail and Elmer leaned over too.

After a long silence Haylestone looked at McNiff.

"You've had experience on cable ships. How d'you get it off?"

"I was only an engineer. That was seamen's work." He rubbed one cold leg against the other. "You navigated onto it. You'd better navigate off it."

Haylestone rammed his hands down into his pea-jacket pockets. He was casting about for an inspiration, a method of disengaging himself from that infernal serpent, when his eye caught something.

"What's that?"

He was standing high above McNiff looking out across the water. All hands looked.

There, beyond the fairway buoy, steaming up off Chebucto Head, was a vessel.

"*Ethel B!*" someone exclaimed.

Haylestone leapt round.

"Merv! . . . Merv!" He had to repeat himself to draw the mate's attention from the object moving stealthily over the ruffled sea against the tall, black cliffs of the headland four miles away.

"Merv. Let go that anchor. Stop it with the first shackle on deck . . . Elmer, get a buoy and ten fathoms of rope . . . and fetch a sledge hammer. That'll do, Angus. Forget your motor. Jump down to the engine room and stand by."

McNiff started to speak, something about navigating, but the roar of the chain going out drowned what he had to say.

They put the stopper on the anchor chain and Elmer secured the buoy-rope to it. Hiram Haylestone was playing his last card. He'd slip his anchor with fifteen fathoms of chain and buoy it so that it could easily be located and not lost on the bottom for ever, even though it held an octopus to its bosom. Then he'd finish the race.

But by the time they were ready to break the chain the *Ethel B* was up to Neverfail buoy. Then with a clang of the sledge the pin shot out of the shackle and the chain fell apart.

"Let go the stopper," Haylestone roared. Quail,

quicker than usual, kicked it out and the end of the chain rattled down the hawse-pipe with the rope. Elmer threw the buoy over.

In an instant all was quiet. Just a little can buoy with a spar sticking up floated on the agitated water.

Back in the wheel-house Haylestone rang the telegraph for full speed. Ed swung the wheel over to port and the *Maid of Jeddore* headed out into the fairway. But with all McNiff's efforts below and Haylestone's urgings from above, by the time she reached the buoyed channel she was in the wake of the *Ethel B* – in the tail of her wake. The two vessels entered harbour like naval ships in line ahead, Haylestone glaring at the stern of the vessel commanded by that man from Clam Harbour.

As Haylestone came out of the mess-room after a difficult breakfast, his well-trained eye sighted a grey little man standing on the wharf. Captain Ezekiel Klogg might have been examining the *Maid's* rugged hull planking or he might have been scrutinizing the cargo coming out of the hold. It was hard to say. Anyway, he was whistling a tune. Haylestone crossed to the side and descended to the wharf.

The first thing he did was to congratulate Klogg on winning the race. After a brief exchange about falling freight rates Klogg pointed to the empty hawse-pipe.

"Where's your starboard anchor, Hiram?" His forehead was puckered now.

"Be glad to explain it to you, Zeke," Haylestone replied affably. "Come aboard."

In his cabin Haylestone poured out two half glasses of rum and put the bottle on the table.

"You were asking where my starboard anchor was. You'd naturally be concerned, I know, Zeke. It's yours, of course."

He held up his glass. Klogg did the same. "Good freights," Haylestone said. "Good freights," Klogg replied. They downed their drinks.

"I'll tell you, Zeke," Haylestone went on. "I was up off Chebucto Head that early – long before you – and it was that thick o' fog, I had to anchor, as you saw. Well, when it cleared after dawn I tried to heave in but that blasted windlass motor of mine was deader than a salted cod. In spite of what Angus McNiff – a clever engineer – tried to do it wouldn't move. And then seeing you sliding in I just had to get underway and try to beat you. So I just slipped the chain and buoyed it. It's right there handy for you, Zeke." Haylestone leaned forward and put his hand on Klogg's shoulder. "You can pick it up as you go out and you'll get fifteen fathoms of chain with it, gratis. I'll give you that."

With the slower and expanded repetition of the episode, during which the level of the bottle fell like an ebbing tide, the suspicious Klogg began to come round. He held his glass up to the light of the port once more, looked at the dark red liquid and, at last, agreed. He also accepted the suggestion that he would pass over his little anchor to Haylestone because, as Haylestone said, "Although it'll be practically no use in holding my vessel to the ground except in a dead calm, it'll satisfy the law about having two anchors."

Captain Haylestone had the story later on of what happened when Klogg sailed two days later bound for Canso. One of the *Ethel B's* hands, a nephew of Merv Quail, related it to his uncle who passed it on to Haylestone.

On his way out Captain Ezekiel Klogg stopped his vessel inside Thrumcap Shoal to pick up his newly-won anchor. His confidence in Haylestone rose when he found the buoy at once. They winched the rope in, got hold of the chain and commenced heaving in. Klogg now began to realize what a very heavy anchor it was. Doubts began to assail him as to the wisdom of exchanging his for this one. It took all the power the *Ethel B* had to heave it up. But when it broke surface Klogg, who was directing operations personally from the forecastle, saw that it was fouled.

In his preoccupation he had paid no attention to the launch, a heavy work-boat, which had been idling against the tide some distance away. Now he became suddenly aware of its powerful motor chugging towards him.

The launch churned the water as it pulled up close under the bow of the *Ethel B*. Three men were standing up in it, balancing to the slight rock. They spoke among themselves as they gazed at the anchor just above the surface of the water, and at the rope-like object stretched over the flukes. Then one of them in a heavy raincoat looked up.

"Cap'n?"

"Yes," Klogg answered slowly, leaning over, figuring the launch might be a local pirate ready to bargain for the removal of the rope.

"Just hold it like that," the man said, raising his hand. The boat's engine kicked over once and two of the men had hold of Klogg's ground-tackle and began prying at it.

"Lay off there!" Klogg bawled. "Get your hands off that rope. What the hell d'you think you're doing? Shove off or I'll let my anchor go, chain and all on top of you."

The men pushed their boat off.

"Cap'n," said the man in the raincoat. "We're from the Canadian Cable Corporation and we've been looking for a break in the trans-Atlantic telephone cable. Now we've got it. A lot of circuits out. What have you been trying to do with it? Hack it in two?"

Klogg hung heavily on the bulwark rail, his eyes working alternately between the cable on the anchor and the men in the launch. One of them, he noticed, had a camera. Then he raised himself and cleared his throat.

"This isn't my anchor. I just happened to . . . "

"That's all right, Cap'n."

"It belongs to . . . "

"Okay, okay. I'll come aboard while my launch goes in to report and start arrangements for the repair job."

Zeke Klogg vaguely watched the boat putter down the lee side to put the man aboard. Then he looked over the bow again.

"Hiram Haylestone!" he shouted down at the cable, as though expecting to get a message through it. "You . . . You . . . You and your blasted navigating!"

He became incoherent after that.

# Rum Compass

The man stepped from the wharf onto the broad bulwark rail and down onto the deck of the *Maid of Jeddore* as though he were used to boarding vessels. To Captain Hiram Haylestone, who was standing on the fore deck, he seemed to carry himself with uncommon confidence in spite of the heavy fibre case which burdened his left arm. The crew suspended work and stood like pointers watching a falling pheasant. A stranger boarding in an outport was unusual, especially if he had the markings of a city slicker.

"Morning, Capt'n," the man said, holding out his hand which was slowly accepted. "Been trying to catch you in port for a long time. Important news for you."

"Important news?" queried Captain Haylestone, looking down wonderingly at the smartly pressed young man, a picture of vigour.

The stranger lowered the fibre case to the deck of the little coastal trader and applied therapy to his left hand with his right.

"My name's Bob Doggett. You don't know me."

"Sure don't."

"You've been sailing on the coast for many years, Capt'n Haylestone, and are one of Nova Scotia's best known skippers. You've been in and out of its ports since before I was born, I'm sure, and no doubt you think you're familiar with every rock along the shore and the shape of every harbour, the position of all the buoys in the channels and . . . "

"I *think* I am . . . familiar?" Haylestone interrupted loudly. He had detached himself from the scarred bulwark. His visitor grasped his fibre case again and started to back from the oncoming giant.

"Who are you, coming aboard my vessel telling me I think I'm familiar with the rocks and harbours? Who the hell are you?"

"Bob Doggett, sir."

"I know. You told me that. What else are you?"

"I'll tell you, sir." He could not move his case any further away because it was up against the hatch coaming. So he left it alone. "I'll tell you at once. I'm the representative of Marine Technical and Electronic Devices Corporation and I'm here to show you the very instrument you need to navigate your vessel safely through the dangerous waters bordering our shores."

"I've heard that line before."

It had been a while since the hands standing around had been treated to the kind of entertainment they liked best.

"It's radar, Capt'n Haylestone. You, of course, are acquainted with the most modern navigational contrivance known to the seafarer today; the device," and he bent down and unlatched the fibre case, opened the lid and displayed a cathode ray tube, like a round television face. "The device that can show you your way in fog, mist, falling snow and heavy rainstorms and take you through the black of night, without fear of grounding or collision with another ship."

"Belay it, me lad." If there had been a cliff at the head of the wharf there would have been as good an echo from the voice of the master of the *Maid of Jeddore* as ever came back from the 'Indian Love Call.' "I am acquainted – at a distance. Seen other vessels with that gadget. But don't try to tell me I want it. How do you think I've been finding my way for nigh on twenty-five years round these parts; aye, and as far north as Cape Chidley and south to the West Indies? Eh?"

"Without radar, Capt'n."

"Yes, without radar, young fella. Same as we get along without running water coming out of half a dozen fancy faucets aboard this boat."

The salesman stood his ground firmly. "You know, you are one of the only coasting masters without radar."

"I know."

"And statistics show that masters can't afford to be without this inexpensive adjunct, Capt'n."

"Expensive junk! You'd better pack up and take your suitcase ashore, Mr. Doggett. I don't need radar."

Doggett apparently knew when "the hard sell" had failed. He thanked the captain cordially for listening and took his gear ashore.

Everyone was surprised soon after dinner to see the representative of Marine Technical and Electronics coming aboard again. His proposal now was to be permitted to set up the equipment temporarily and have the captain try it out; no charge, no obligation. "Purely on a trial basis. You won't even have to make a down payment on it."

For a good ten minutes Haylestone paced up and down the fore deck with his hands behind his back while the cargo was being loaded. He glanced occasionally aloft. Doggett squatted on a bollard ready to apply the "soft sell." Suddenly the rhythmic tread came to a halt.

"All right. Stick it in . . . temporarily mind you. I'll see how unnecessary it is. But you've got to come along for the voyage and work it."

Doggett had risen. "Well, thank you, Capt'n. But how long are you going away for?"

Haylestone told him about a week, just to Newfoundland. "Leaving tomorrow evening, probably."

With some hesitation the salesman thought he might be able to go and went off to telephone his head office in Halifax.

## RUM COMPASS

No sooner had the *Maid of Jeddore* cleared the bay than she became enveloped in the fog which had been lying off the south-east coast for days. But Captain Hiram Haylestone was used to it. He set his wooden double-ender on a north-easterly course and shouted down to Mervin Quail, who was hosing down the deck, to hoist the mainsail – the wind was astern, a regular fog breeze, and the sail would help to steady her. He took the wheel himself and sent the helmsman down. It took four to hoist the sail.

Bob Doggett was fiddling about with the radar which he had installed on the port side of the wheelhouse with a short temporary mast and antenna above it. "Coast's showing up clearly, Cap," he announced at length.

The captain might not have heard him. He looked up from the compass and gazed out the open window, his black-browed eyes searching the damp grey curtain beyond the bow. When Ed came back to the wheel he stepped aside and studied the fog from the starboard window.

"Shore's all along the port side," Doggett said, his eyes and most of his nose down in the heavy rubber cowl which fitted tightly over the radar display.

Captain Haylestone examined his cigar critically and tidied up his long black moustache with the knuckles of his left hand. "Course it's to port," he grunted.

"A boat or something ahead, I think" Doggett remarked slowly. But the captain merely reached up and pulled the cord of the fog horn. It made a long deep-throated blare.

The following wind brought the sound of the diesel motor closer – as well as the oily flakes of soot. It made hearing difficult.

Suddenly a shrieking whistle pierced the fog close to the bow. Almost instantly Haylestone saw a huge red object dead ahead. Before the ear-splitting noise stopped he had thrust at a spoke of the wheel beside him. Ed caught the meaning and was tugging the wheel to port.

The whistle stopped with a diaphonic jerk. Haylestone threw the telegraph to full astern. The funnel made two more putts; then there was a sickening crash. The vessel shuddered and heeled over to port. Haylestone rang "stop." The boat righted herself and the great red buoy, as tall as Haylestone's bridge, slithered down the starboard side and disappeared into the fog astern.

They had run down the Lahave whistle buoy moored three miles out from West Ironbound Island.

"Lower the mainsail," Haylestone shouted to the mate. "And tell the chief to sound the bilges." As Merv Quail sent a couple of hands aft he leaned over the rail forward but could not see the extent of the damage. Haylestone said they would look at her side from the hold first.

The men hauled the tarpaulins back, threw the hatch covers off and jumped down onto the cargo. Below, they pulled cases and bales back from the starboard side. They could hear water running in as they ripped away the splintered inner lining of the hull. Between a pair of frames they found three timbers stove in on the waterline.

They knocked the timbers back a bit, stuffed canvas into the cracks and split wood and nailed planks against the fracture. This staunched the main tide but she still leaked badly. The chief engineer confirmed the inflow; Angus McNiff's big pump was already labouring with more than it could contend.

Haylestone decided to attack the injury from outboard. They slung a wooden hatch cover over the side with steadying lines around the bow and under the keel, and Merv Quail was lashed onto it flat and lowered to the water's edge. Then Elmer was lowered in an upside down position to pass oakum to the mate and hold his tools. They were both ducked often in the freezing water as the boat rolled, though fortunately not too deeply, but Quail drove enough oakum into the half shattered planking with his caulking hammer to keep the inflow down.

They got under way again: Haylestone had no intention of turning back although Angus McNiff had his doubts.

The next afternoon they jogged along off the Cape Breton shore. The fog had dispersed for the moment. Haylestone had been vaguely watching a fast ship crossing ahead making towards the Cabot Straits. Doggett was still there in the wheel-house periodically peering into his "machine" as Haylestone now spoke of it when he had to. Bob Doggett had remarked a number of times on the graphic picture the coastline presented in the radar but the captain had taken no notice.

"That ship there," Doggett murmured from the lightshielding cowl, "is three and a quarter miles away."

Haylestone looked sharply at the stooping figure. He was surprised that Doggett had measured the distance as accurately as he could with his eye.

"Land on the port hand," Doggett intoned, "Bears from three-two-oh degrees to two-two-five. Nearest point abeam four and a half miles. Have a look, Cap," Doggett said brightly, persuasively, lifting his head.

"What the hell sort of lingo is that, three-two-oh to two-two-five? Navy?"

"Bearings, Cap," Doggett answered solicitously.

"Don't understand highfalutin stuff like that."

Doggett glanced into the hood. "About north-west to south-west."

"Now you're talking sense."

After glowering at the ship in the distance and tugging his beard the captain slowly moved round behind the wheel and cursorily glanced into the radar. He sniffed loudly as he stepped back and looked into the helmsman's compass. "No wandering off the course, now," he said to Elmer at the wheel, who had heard the admonition many times.

"Have another look, Cap," Doggett almost begged.

Haylestone surveyed the instrument as though it were a decaying piece of whale blubber offensively occupying valuable space. Then he pushed his peaked cap back, leaned down and pressed his face against the elliptical mask. He remained in this attitude for some time, perhaps two minutes.

"You reckon that outline on the left is the coast?"

"Certainly is."

"Where's that ship you said you could see?"

"That blip, that small mark – a bit to the right in front, beyond the three-mile circle."

After another examination Haylestone straightened up, looked down intently at the "machine," then went out the door and down the ladder. He paced up and down the deck and presently his thoughts shifted to the damaged hull and the ultimate expense of repair.

The *Maid of Jeddore* chugged across the Gulf of St. Lawrence peacefully to the sound of the diesel motor and the bilge pump and before dawn rounded Cape Race. Bob Doggett continued to announce his radar observations of the headlands as they worked up the Newfoundland coast but Haylestone only became really impressed when he was negotiating the passage between Baccalieu Island and the mainland. Doggett was reporting bearings astoundingly accurately.

They did several ports in Conception Bay: Topsail and Foxtrap, Uppergully and Harbour Grace; then they went round to Heart's Content in Trinity Bay and finally discharged the last of their freight at Old Perlican.

Whenever they were at a wharf they examined the split timbers in the hull. Haylestone and the mate would take it in turns to go down a rope ladder and try to recaulk the fractures. They could not apply paint because the hull was always wet. It was an ugly looking gash. Angus McNiff had to run his bilge pump continuously except while lying quietly in harbours. He liked to comment about it. "Water's gaining. If she strikes hard weather and her hull works, it'll pour in. Expensive accident that."

Haylestone knew only too well that the profit of the voyage was going to be taken by the shipyard.

It was at Old Perlican that Bob Doggett made his recommendation. The *Maid* was lying at anchor slinging cargo down into boats alongside.

"Your compass, Cap," Doggett opened in his best sales voice. "It isn't graduated consecutively all the way round to three hundred and sixty degrees."

"No," Haylestone agreed.

"It should be, shouldn't it?"

"Why?"

"It's old fashioned."

"It's a fine magnetic compass. Given me good service for many years and has no deviation." They were sitting in the mess-room finishing dinner.

"Yes, I'm sure," Doggett accepted. "Its just that it's out-of-date to have it graduated only from nought to ninety between the cardinal points. It must be very inconvenient at times and it will become more so with the advancement of science."

"So I've noticed," Haylestone reluctantly acknowledged.

"Why don't you let me renumber the card for you," Doggett offered.

"Renumber the card!" Haylestone exclaimed. The thought shocked him. Yet it was a bright idea; modern.

"As of course you know, Cap, no navigational device now-a-days is graduated by the old points of the compass. We haven't seen that at Marine Tec and Electronics for years. And with radar you need the three-hundred-and-sixty system."

"This new age of seeing things when they're invisible, steering a vessel without a man at the wheel as I hear some do, astronauts and all; what's the maritime world coming to? And now we've got to box the compass in a new-fangled way. That's sac . . . sacrilege, Bob; that's what it is; sacrilege!"

"I won't scratch anything out. Just write the additional numbers from ninety to three-sixty."

After some feeble resistance to Doggett's penetrating logic, Haylestone finally acceded to the renumbering being done while they were at anchor in Old Perlican Harbour. It wouldn't take long, Doggett said. Haylestone knew Bob was a smart fellow, very likable too; the kind of lad he would like to have had for a son. Besides, he had served a spell in the navy and was obviously highly educated.

They went up to the wheel-house followed slowly by the mate who had listened to some of the conversation. Haylestone gingerly took the compass out of the binnacle, having directed Doggett in its release from the gimbles, his own hands being too large to get at the screws. He set it carefully on the deck and they both got down on their knees, Doggett applying the screwdriver to the glass cover while Haylestone held the compass bowl. When it came off Doggett lifted the card from the central pivot.

On the chart table in Haylestone's cabin they fingered the thin circular metallic card and waited for it to dry. It did not take long; the alcohol evaporated quickly. Haylestone hung his peaked cap on the door knob so that he could observe more closely while Doggett got out his ball point. Quail leaned against the bunk smoking his pipe and took cognizance of events as they occurred.

There was a narrow margin immediately outside the ring of existing numerals and in this margin Doggett started to etch the figures at every ten degrees. He had to be careful because the vessel was rocking slightly on the ground swell which came into the harbour. As he got around to 180, his tongue hugging his upper lip, Haylestone wondered if the ink would run when put back in the alcohol, but Bob said it would not if they dried it well.

"We'll harden it up over the galley stove," Haylestone said, which Doggett thought was a good idea.

The numbers were well sketched in, Doggett thickening them with his aggressive ball point until he reached 350. Then they all stood back and admired the artistry.

"How about drawing a dolphin in the middle, Bob," Quail asked.

"Can't draw," said Bob. "Can you?"

"Spare-me-days, no! Maybe Hiram can."

"Me draw! We've done enough already. Down to the galley with it. Give it to me, Bob. Can't afford to drop it."

They were up again in fifteen minutes.

"Stand by with the screwdriver, Bob," Haylestone ordered as he bent over the compass bowl on the deck of the wheel-house. A moment later Quail, entering by the starboard door, found the captain down like a Mohammedan on his prayer mat. He seemed to be choking.

"Looks like part of the stuff's gone." He rubbed a huge hand over a discoloured circle on the deck around the bowl. "Doggett. Where's Doggett?"

Doggett acknowledged his presence.

"Here. Damn my buttons! The alcohol's spilt out of the bowl with the vessel's motion. Why in hell didn't you bottle it, or pour it off into a bucket or something."

"You didn't tell me to," the draughtsman answered, the lightness of his voice falling like a rain drop on a fog horn.

Haylestone stood up. "Alcohol. Where are we going to find alcohol? Blast it! Why did this have to happen! Merv. Alcohol."

"We ain't got any . . . unless Angus has."

"Bob." He shot a shrivelling glance at the instigator of the plot. "Don't stand there like you were going to fall off the yard arm. Go and see if Angus McNiff has any alcohol."

Doggett turned but stepped on a folding stool

which leaped up at his ankle like a snarling dog. He shook his foot free and the stool half rose, then collapsed against the compass bowl which rocked and gently fell over.

The words which escaped Haylestone's lips made even Merv Quail wince.

Doggett righted the bowl, but its contents were running under the flag locker and the wheel-house smelt like the emergency ward of a hospital. Haylestone relieved himself somewhat by picking up the stool and heaving it overboard.

McNiff had none of what was wanted and expressed himself indignantly to that effect.

"We'll have to send ashore for it," Haylestone told Quail.

The mate went down, the men swung the boat over, and Elmer took the oars and pulled to the beach.

In twenty minutes he was back with grim news. "Wouldn't give me none. Asked in the store – there's only one – fishermen in there. The man says, 'You asking me for alcohol?' 'Yes,' I says. Then he says, 'Where ye to?' 'Halifax,' I says. So he asks me how many crew we got. I says, 'Seven men and a Newfoundlander,' thinking that would please him but it sure didn't – nor the fishermen."

"We'll have to use gin, Cap," said Doggett.

"Gin! There's no gin aboard this vessel. Who'd drink gin?"

"Well, some other alcoholic beverage then. Got some white rum?"

"White! Course not."

But Haylestone was brightening up. "Got plenty of Schreecher's. That's rich alcoholic stuff." And he went back into his cabin abaft the wheel-house and came out with two bottles.

"Come on. We're late leaving now." The freight had been discharged and the boats had left. "Get her filled up now," Haylestone instructed. "Put it up on the table here, Bob."

They poured nearly two bottles of Schreecher's Newfoundland into the compass bowl but it was quickly, though silently, realized that Schreecher's was a very dark rum. Haylestone felt like a man who had poured coffee on his porridge.

Doggett placed the card on the pivot and they watched to see if the ink would run. It was difficult to tell. It was like trying to detect the features of a Moslem damsel beneath her veil. And the view was not enhanced when they screwed the glass cover down and a large air bubble appeared under it.

"You didn't put in enough rum, Bob," Haylestone said. "Unscrew the cover and we'll top it up."

"Shouldn't there be a spigot somewhere to let the last of the air out and fill it tight?"

"I've never seen one in this compass."

They looked underneath and all round the compass but apparently the captain was right, there was no spigot.

They went through this process of debubbling twice but the only improvement they could make was to break the big bubble into several small ones, which Bob Doggett said reminded him of splitting the atom. By straining their eyes to the utmost they could see the figures; in fact, they were a little clearer through the air bubbles, and in a certain deflection of light they could tell a 2 from a 4. Quail said it was a pity it hadn't been done in luminous paint but he, personally, was glad he could see the big black mark like the ace of spades denoting the north cardinal point.

There was nothing for it but to go out to sea in a condition which the underwriters of marine insurance would have described as an unseaworthy state.

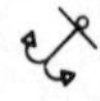

In daylight they had the coast to steer by, but this was difficult because when they left the little harbour that afternoon it was slashing with rain. Bob Doggett could tell the distance off shore by his radar but that did not help the helmsman when he could not see it.

Haylestone kept the *Maid* close in. But at times he had trouble seeing the cliffs and wooded hills himself, even at half a mile – the heavy banks of rain frequently blotted them out. He managed to sight Breakheart Point and this enabled him to round the end of the peninsula. The rain then lessened as they got clear of the high land and he was able to negotiate the channel inside Baccalieu Island. Night came as he emerged into the unobstructed ocean.

Haylestone stopped his vessel and waited. Towards midnight he saw the steaming lights of a ship coming down the coast and as soon as she was passed he started up and followed her. All the helmsman had to do was to follow her stern light.

This scheme went well until the steamer turned west at Cape Race. The *Maid of Jeddore* had to go south. Now came the test: to make Halifax 500 miles away, under a sky devoid of heavenly bodies, without inadvertently sighting Bermuda or Greenland – and all this with a badly leaking boat. Never did seamen think that their eyes would grow weary of looking at rum. But sometimes when the movement of the vessel made the compass shudder the bubbles provided a momentary confirmation of the course.

Doggett's radar did not pick up the Nova Scotia coast and, in any case, Haylestone had lost his interest in the "machine" and was bad tempered. He did however find the Canso Bank with soundings.

By the afternoon of the third day he reckoned he had run his distance to Halifax and missed it. He therefore followed his old practice of heading directly into the land hoping to pick up a region of the coast he could recognize. But it was dull and misty and he would have to get well in to see much of the land. After running for two hours, a report came from Doggett that he could see a ship ahead in his spectrum, or possibly two ships close together.

Haylestone grunted. To him the instrument was now about as useful as the hole in the hull.

Soon, however, he could see a tug towing something. On closing the distance he saw it was a naval tug with a large target at the end of a very long tow rope. Haylestone noted that it was 4.30 and figured the tug was in-bound. Firing practice would have been completed. He had never seen naval ships doing anything after 5 o'clock except berthing themselves comfortably alongside the dockyard. So he fell in on the weather side of the target and jogged along at the same pace. The two would inevitably bring him to the harbour mouth, albeit slowly.

It was while Haylestone was lighting a new cigar, feeling a sense of relaxation for the first time for days, that he heard a swish close over the wheelhouse. He ducked out, looked up, but saw nothing.

Then he heard the tug blasting off with her whistle and noticed a variety of coloured flags on her yard arm halyards. Two further swishing effects whistled close overhead followed by distant thunder. Then there was a ping and the top of his own foremast fell to the deck.

"Shooting!" Doggett shouted. "Firing practice!"

Haylestone had already tumbled to the manifestation and ordered the wheel swung hard aport.

Before the *Maid of Jeddore* could respond to her rudder a distinct thud was felt against the hull. Haylestone leapt to the starboard side.

There, bobbing in the sea was a black cigar-shaped object with a rounded nose.

"Torpedo!" Doggett ejaculated, looking over.

"Full astern," Haylestone hurled back at Ambrose at the wheel. He did not take his eyes off the odious projectile. "Fish it aboard, Merv," he yelled down to the mate.

Merv Quail, who had appeared on deck at the fall of the masthead, had also reached the side and was calling for grapnels.

Bob Doggett spoke up as though quoting from a book. "When the enemy is firing at a defenceless ship, turn away at best speed and present the narrowest target."

Captain Hiram Haylestone felt as if he were back in the old days on rum row, battling it out with the coast guard. "I'll have that dang torpedo even if I get the other mast shot away!"

With a bit of manoeuvring they fished up the torpedo and laid it carefully in the scuppers. They knew it was unarmed; a homing peace-time practice job. Doggett said it had about reached the end of its run. Then Haylestone made full use of the radar on his own initiative.

"Where's that warship, Bob?"

"Bearing oh-five-five, Cap, three miles."

"Steer oh-five-five. And watch the compass Ambrose, even if your eyeballs come out." He murmured something about presenting the narrowest target but going towards the enemy. Like Farragut at Mobile Bay, he damned the torpedoes and went ahead.

All hands on deck were keeping a lookout now. They could hear the tug hooting away on her whistle as they left her astern, flags flying. Doggett shouted, "Two miles." Then there was a resumption of the thunder.

"Steer for that gunfire, Ambrose," the captain roared.

"There she is," shouted the cook whose eyes were better trained than the young hands'.

A dark smudge had suddenly emerged from the mist and quickly resolved itself into a sleek grey warship.

Firing ceased.

Next they saw a series of flashes obviously coming from a powerful projector.

"Signalling," Doggett said knowledgeably.

"Take no notice," Haylestone answered. "They ought to know we don't bother with that stuff."

It took ten minutes at McNiff's best speed to reach the destroyer. Captain Haylestone swung the *Maid of Jeddore* onto a parallel course, starboard side towards her, when he came within a hundred yards of the slowing warship. Then he went out onto the wing of the bridge.

"Captain ahoy." His voice reverberated over the waters of the firing area of the great naval base.

After a short delay and a variety of static noises a cultivated voice spoke through a loud-hailer. "Captain here. What do you mean by getting in my way while I'm carrying out a shoot?"

"On a defenceless vessel. You're in *my* way."

"Get going please. Where are you bound?"

"Halifax, of course – for repairs and to see the admiral."

There was no immediate response. He saw the commander apparently conferring with staff officers beside him. Haylestone took another deep breath.

"You see that foremast – if you know what a foremast is?" He pointed aloft. "You shot the top off."

He turned his head. "Merv, show the navy the top of the pole."

The hands on the fore deck held the jagged-ended spar up to view.

"Expensive things masts," he bellowed. He had no need to cup his hands around his mouth. "And look at my hull under the anchor. You torpedoed my vessel. Bloody near drove a hole through her. Expensive things hulls. It'll cost you and the admiral plenty to repair that."

The clicking of a volume control came across the intervening space. "Torpedoed you?" an incredulous metallic voice queried. "What do you mean . . . torpedoed you?"

Haylestone leaned over the bridge rail again. "Up with the torpedo, Merv."

The men ducked down, rolled the projectile out of the scuppers and up-ended it on the hatch. It rather resembled a small space rocket on its launching pad, Haylestone thought.

He waited. After a minute the voice came again.

"I'll send a boat over for the torpedo. Thank you, Captain."

Haylestone heard the shrill pipe and a bo'sun-like voice resounding over the destroyer's deck, "Away seaboat's crew," and he saw men running. He swung round.

"Lower that thing into the hold, Merv."

Then he took three strides to the wheel-house, threw the telegraph handle hard down to full ahead.

Outside, he filled his lungs with good Nova Scotian air once more.

"Never mind, Captain. I'll give it to the admiral when he comes aboard after he's repaired my hull and stepped a new mast – at government expense."

Then he gave the telegraph a double ring – emergency full speed for McNiff.

"Can you see Chebucto Head and the harbour entrance in that radar of yours, Bob?" he asked.

"Right ahead, Cap."

"Steady as you go, Ambrose," Captain Hiram Haylestone ordered the helmsman, "and don't get blinded with the rum.

The fog thinned as they drew closer to the land and Doggett's predictions proved to be correct.

"Bob," Haylestone said suddenly.

"Cap."

"Bob. One day I'm going to buy a radar. Guess you've shown me. Can't do it yet awhile though. Costly gadgets, radars – like masts, only more." He looked at Doggett. "Don't worry, my boy, I'll come to you when I'm ready."

# Special Cargo

The last consignment of cargo was to be loaded at what was known to the small tonnage fraternity as Shultz Wharf. Oil-smeared barges lay against it and a bulky row boat clung to its piles underneath as the *Maid of Jeddore* came alongside after threading her way across New York's Hudson River. In the fading light the decrepit wooden sheds blended naturally with the black river water and warehouse-and-chimney background of Weehawken.

Captain Hiram Haylestone came ashore and looked up and down. As he commenced impatiently pacing the quay's uneven planking, he began to experience a feeling of uncertainty about the wisdom of coming to this deserted, grimy wharf. It bore in on him that he knew almost nothing about the consignor of the special cargo. He started to question whether he had fully understood that fellow Brass' verbal arrangement back in Halifax, or if the wretched man had messed it up somewhere. He kicked a rotting bollard securing a tarry mooring rope. Then he spotted a man turning the corner onto Shultz Wharf. His shadow, cast by the bare electric light at the end, lengthened as he approached.

"Captain Haylestone?" asked the man as he came up.

"Of course, of course."

"You sound like you're in a hurry."

"I'm not here for the benefit of my health," retorted Haylestone.

"You waiting for something then? Cargo perhaps?" said the fat little man whose most prominent features, apart from his stomach, were his fin-like ears.

"If you're the man who has my cargo I'll take it. Your name Murphy?"

"No, Finestone. It's the same thing. Your men ready to take it aboard?"

"Soon as you are."

Mr. Finestone unlocked the door of the dilapidated shed and swung it back. He said he had the key from Mr. Shultz. Haylestone roared down at the deck of his vessel for the mate.

Mate Mervin Quail and the men examined the stack of freight critically – the men had to carry it. After viewing from every angle what seemed to be slabs of stone, Merv Quail passed his hand over the top of the pile and expressed himself briefly: "Marble monuments!"

One of the crew muttered, "Gravestones." Someone said, "Heavy stuff," and the air cleared a little.

"Get it aboard," Haylestone ordered. "Can't hang around here all night."

The men were strong but they seemed to display superhuman strength when they picked up the first headstone and carried it lightly over to the dockside. Great satisfaction registered on the face of the man with the fin-like ears.

"This style we call our 'two-by-four': it's two feet by four feet; width eight inches. Try lifting it, Captain."

Haylestone reached down, grasped one end of a monument and rose with it as though he were picking up a dried codfish.

"Brass was right," he observed.

"Course he was right."

Haylestone dropped the memorial to the deceased and it bounced appreciably.

As the men shifted more of the cargo to the quayside and swung it into the hold with the forward derrick, under the watchful eye of the mate, Haylestone was regaled by Mr. Finestone on the advantages of these particular "stones." It became evident to Haylestone that the shipper was also the enthusiastic manufacturer.

"Plastic gravestones," he was saying. "Most modern invention in the world today." He explained it was his name that gave him the angle. "Finestone. A mighty fine stone, see. I'm expanding my sales every day. You can't tell them from Italian marble – long as you don't handle them. Durable as hell. Weather anything and always look like new. Easy to inscribe. Easy to erect too, and no maintenance."

Haylestone noticed they were moulded with a kind of blister on the base, presumably to encourage a perpendicular posture forever before the elements of their final environment – the manufacturer must have made a study of the falling factor of ordinary stones.

"They sell here under the trade name of Murphy's Monuments," Mr. Finestone added.

"Why Murphy?" asked Haylestone, his heavy black eyebrows drawn together.

"Finestone's Tombstones ain't easy to say and it's too synonymous. Murphy's a good name; same as Murphy's Beds; and they're just as light to handle; hollow in the middle, you know."

The captain thought of Haylestone's Gravestones, which they now were temporarily becoming, but put it out of his mind.

Mr. Finestone parted with his merchandise on a friendly basis and did not offer a bill of lading. The captain did not expect one.

Angus McNiff sat on the after hatch rolling a cigarette and sourly contemplating the doorway to his engine room. The cool Atlantic breeze, blowing across the inert coastal trader was drying his sweating chest. Over him stood Haylestone, his tall frame swaying easily to the vessel's movement in the hummocky sea. He spoke to his engineer in gentler terms than he was accustomed to.

"You've been down below puttering around that engine for an hour. What the hell's the matter with it? How long are you going to be?"

McNiff glanced up at the black-bearded face beneath the salt-stained peaked cap, then removed the loose threads of tobacco extending from the ends of his thin cigarette.

"Lookit Angus," the captain tried again, "how long . . ."

"I'm resting," the chief interrupted and fished his worn brass lighter out of his pants' pocket.

"I can see that all right. But it isn't as though you were in the habit of busting up the engine. How long will it be?"

Angus McNiff leant to leeward a little and struck the flint wheel of the lighter he was fondling. "I don't know how long it'll take me. At least one valve spring's gone."

Haylestone was in rather an anxious state of mind. "See that swell," he said, looking over the dipping rail. McNiff ignored the smooth rollers as he got to his feet. "Sou'-easterly. Strong breeze coming. Maybe a late summer storm. I don't want the vessel to be lying here like a dead haddock, unable to turn her screw, rolling her guts out when that comes. Think of those 'stones' down below. They'll be charging across the hold and getting bashed up."

McNiff's move towards the engine room door was suddenly arrested. "I don't want to think of them 'stones.' I don't like them. It's probably because of the monuments that my engine's giving trouble. My engine, Hiram . . . your 'stones'!" He turned sideways and lifted his short legs over the high weather doorstep and disappeared below.

Up on the bridge deck Haylestone pulled a new cigar from the pocket of his once brass-buttoned blue vest which he was wearing over his turtle-necked sweater, and removed the end with his teeth, disposing of it to leeward. He was thinking as he paced the small area.

The important thing of the voyage was to have the gravestones delivered to Mr. Brass in good order and condition, and without the customs moving in. But Mr. Brass had said he would see to that. The risk was "practically non-existent" he had said. Brass had been forced to import in this way because of the unfair duty on plastics: headstones and vault plaques were manufactured only in the United States. And there was, as he had explained, a ready market for such merchandise, particularly in the country: they could be sold more cheaply net (less duty) than cut granite or marble. It was to be on a trial basis; high freight rate and small risk. Haylestone pondered the question.

Suddenly he became more sensitive to the welfare of the stones in the hold. He had to brace himself against several distinctly heavy rolls as the heightening waves before the storm passed under the keel. Glancing to the south-east he observed a significant line of cumulo-nimbus clouds. Soon he had to take shelter in the lee of the wheel-house against the strong gusts of wind and rain. And in the tumult he saw rather than heard the mate come up and stand beside him, his oilskin coat glistening in the watery westering sun.

Haylestone relieved himself of a couple of technical remarks. "Angus can't get his blasted engine to go. Claims it's something to do with the cargo – and he looks at me like I'd shot a ruddy albatross."

"Me too," Merv Quail announced.

The unusually rapid retort from the mate drew a quick glance from Haylestone. He was surprised to see on the normally tranquil, craggy face, an uncertain and perplexed look as he scowled at the darkening sea.

Quail went on, peering around the wheel-house into the wind. "Sou'-easter. Mighty early in the season for a sou'-easter."

"You stowed the stones tight in among the fertilizer bags, Merv?"

Haylestone waited, then repeated the question louder over a hard squall.

"Yeah," he heard the mate answer.

"What are you bothering about then if they are stowed tight?"

"Hiram," Quail began, "the crew, especially Ambrose and the cook, don't think them stones bode no good for the voyage. And I'm with them." He relapsed into a further study of the weather.

"Is that what you're worried about?"

"Eh?"

"Is that what's worrying you?"

"Yeah. Gravestone cargo. Yeah."

Haylestone felt very much alone. "That doesn't make cricket," he muttered.

First his chief engineer, now his mate; officers who had been with him for years. And the crew were against him. Well, Brass would soon be against him too, he supposed.

The *Maid of Jeddore*, lying off Long Island's Montauk Point, was in that unfortunate position which no seaman likes – powerless, going over on her beam-ends and exposed before the full force of a gale. She could not even run for shelter.

McNiff and the second engineer had worked strenuously down below but it was no good, the boat was wallowing too much, setting the chief on his ear against the cylinder head one moment and almost on his back in the bilges the next. But when he said he was going to pack up, the second engineer seemed to want to stay where he was and work on. It was bright down in the engine room and it was dark and eerie in the hold where he would be forced to go if he were found idle.

Haylestone had ordered an inspection of the fore hold to see if the cargo was shifting or suffering damage. But Mervin Quail said it wasn't any use meddling with that stuff. "Aside from the fertilizer it ain't like any ordinary cargo. It goes where it wants to go and no human hand'll hold it." The husky speech of the Nova Scotian was slow but emphatic.

"Bilge! Utter bilge you're talking, Merv."

He and Haylestone had taken up an oscillating stance in the captain's cabin where the view from the tightly closed port hole revealed two constantly changing scenes, a circle of dark, spume-driven sea, then the leaden overhanging sky. Haylestone had tried to adjust Quail's slow mind.

"What if the monuments are piled up on one side of the hold? That'd constitute a weight which would affect our stability. You know that. Can't afford to have an unstable vessel in these weather conditions."

Merv Quail followed the swing of a coat on a peg like the pendulum of a clock.

"They are liable to be thrown all round in this weather," the captain boomed on, "and all scratched up, maybe." He stopped suddenly and studied the swaying deck of his cabin. "Wonder if they would break in two," he murmured. He finally told the mate to get the hands down at once for the safety of the boat and the protection of valuable cargo.

Quail came to the present. "Men don't like them monuments, Hiram. No one does except you. Leave 'em be."

"Are you refusing to go down?" roared Haylestone.

"Leave 'em be."

"Mister Quail." The import of such a salutation was arresting in itself. "It's mutiny! Mutiny, Mister Quail! Mutiny!"

Had it not been for the tumult of the gale the petrifying words would have been heard down on deck.

"Mutiny," Quail repeated almost inaudibly.

The outcome of this appropriate outburst was that a corner of the forward hatch was opened and two seamen and the cook were sent down. In the process a wave crashing across the deck accompanied them.

In the light of their lamps below, the men saw tombstones lying flat, tombstones half erect, others standing up like guardians over little mounds of fertilizer, now damp as dewy grass. Some stones moved gently to the vessel's motion as though being rocked by unseen hands.

In laying the refractory cargo flat in the tumbling hold and weighting it down with lifeless fertilizer bags, under the direction of Merv Quail, now the Ethiopian slave driver at the pyramids, they managed to make it reasonably secure. As they came up through the hatchway, Elmer said he was surprised the boat didn't turn turtle while they were down there.

Within an hour the storm had abated to the point where McNiff could return to his engine room; and by eleven o'clock that night he had the valve spring replaced. In a dying south-east breeze with the intermittent flash of Montauk light on her port quarter, the *Maid of Jeddore* got under way and steered for Nantucket.

Captain Hiram Haylestone was not a man who wasted ink in the log book. "Crossed the Gulf of Maine," he entered, with the date and time of passing Cape Sable, the southern tip of Nova Scotia, and added the words, "Set course for Halifax."

He now cleaned his old binoculars. Screwing the lenses back he stepped out of the wheel-house to try them for clarity.

He directed his glasses across the ruffled water towards the high land to port which faded now and then as fog patches drifted by. Suddenly he emitted a noise – a surprised kind of grunt. Then added, as though to confirm it, "Well, I'll be caught aback!"

Haylestone was watching a vessel standing out from the land which he recognized with distinct misgivings. He figured she had come out of Negro Harbour. Through his clear binoculars he could see her sharp bow cutting through the quiet sea. She was larger and higher than the ordinary coaster; in fact, rather like a naval ship. As he watched, she bore up to assume a closing course with the *Maid of Jeddore.*

"What d'ye see, Skipper?" asked Elmer at the wheel.

Haylestone let the glasses fall to his chest.

"RCMP."

The statement was made in a flat voice. He again experienced that unusual sensation of friendlessness.

"Police, eh!" the helmsman exclaimed. "Royal Canadian Mounted Police!"

"Wasn't that what I said?" Haylestone snorted. Why did people always like to convey such enthusiasm for things for which he had to bear responsibility?

He noted with irritation the speed with which the police boat was overtaking him. He had always abhorred the element of swiftness in the preventive service. And his attitude towards Inspector Pogson, commanding the vessel, varied according to the burden on his mind. To a less interested party the RCMP boat would have made a stirring sight as she drew abreast a little way off with her flag flying from her gaff, colourful against the rugged Canadian shore in the near distance.

A voice suddenly burst on the waters. Pogson was using a loud-hailer with plenty of volume. The human element behind the mechanical utterance could be recognized as Pogson.

"What ship?" it said.

Haylestone pulled his cigar from his teeth and cupped his hands round his mouth.

"*Maid of Jeddore,*" he bellowed dutifully; then muttered, "As if Pogson doesn't know – he's being official."

"Master's name?"

"Hiram Haylestone." He didn't need a fancy amplifier to throw his voice across.

"Bound?"

"New York to Halifax."

"Any trouble on the voyage?"

Haylestone winced. Trouble? "Engine broke down off Long Island in a gale."

"How is it now?"

"Fair to moderate."

"Want me to stand by in case you need a tow?"

"You can get to hell . . . You can get to Halifax without a worry. So can I."

"What's your cargo?"

Here Haylestone hesitated. And the pause might have been justified as a bank of fog drifted down hiding the police boat. The voice came again in spite of its disembodiment. "What's your cargo?"

"Mostly fertilizer."

That seemed to be all.

But the RCMP did not move on. When the fog cleared ten minutes later the trim, aggressive-looking vessel was still there, about five hundred yards abeam – directly between the *Maid of Jeddore* and the shore.

From then on she disappeared and reappeared as the fog banks came and went, but she remained always in the same relative position. The silence with which it was done; the unnerving coincidence of their meeting; the rather embarrassing position Haylestone felt himself to be in: convoyed for protection against breakdown or under unspoken arrest – he wished he knew which, or what other paternal motive the policeman had – began to make him chew his cigar unmercifully.

But Hiram Haylestone's background had made him a master of initiative and strategy. He might have covered himself with glory had he joined the navy when he was a boy. His weather sense now told him that the fog banks would eventually settle down solidly. He roared for McNiff.

"When I give you a double ring on the telegraph I want all the speed you can lay your engine to. Do you understand?"

"But Hiram . . . "

"No buts. Get down to the machinery and stand by."

"What d'ye want with . . . ?"

Haylestone swung a clenched paw above his head. "So help me!" The vocal strength of the remark was such that he had no need to go further. McNiff was backing his short round figure down the ladder, his eyes riveted on the captain.

Haylestone spoke – gently by comparison – to the man at the wheel. "Bring her closer, Elmer." He jerked his thumb towards the hidden police boat. "But slowly."

The *Maid of Jeddore* imperceptibly reduced the distance to what Haylestone estimated was two hundred yards. His adversary was still invisible. He whistled a short tune: that ought to fix the weather. And the fog rolled down as thick as a hedge. Haylestone seized the handle of the engine room telegraph and gave it two jabs that shivered the column from dial to base.

"Hard aport."

Over Elmer's shoulder he watched the lubber line in the compass move to the left.

"Steady," he ordered when the boat had turned a full ninety degrees.

He flung open the starboard door of the wheel-house and stood like a figurehead in the wing of the little bridge. He hoped his eyes would not pierce the thick grey shield. All he saw was the greenish-white line of the police boat's wake as his own vessel's cut-water surged through it forty seconds after turning.

Haylestone had three miles to go; a little more for safety; say, eighteen or twenty minutes with the engine full out. He came back into the wheel-house and blew down the speaking tube.

"Angus. Put both your feet on the gas. I've slipped Pogson and we're running for shore."

A thin voice came up the pipe. "Aye, aye, Hiram. She's all out. I'll get you there."

The captain's eyes gleamed. "And if I see the rocks too soon I'll want full astern with all your power."

"You'll get it if you ring for it. But don't pile her up!"

Mervin Quail had been wakened from a doze by the sound of the stentorian orders McNiff had received. Emerging from his cabin he was just in time to see the lazy streak of churned water lying across their path. He recognized the manoeuvre.

"Where are you making for, Hiram?" Quail puffed as he reached the bridge.

"Cork Island, if I can find it right. Pogson's abaft the starboard beam there somewhere, sailing on to Halifax." He sniffed hard. "Jump for'ard and clear the anchor. Might need it. And keep your optics peeled for rocks. Sou'-west entrance is strewn with them. Hope the fog doesn't lift before we make it."

"He's got that fog penetrator, ain't he, Hiram? Radar; thing Bob Doggett had."

Haylestone knew it but he did not like to think about that. This was no time to dwell on scientific phenomena. His mind was darting from the set of the tide along the coast and the depth of water beside Cork Island, to what he would do when he arrived in behind the island.

"Rocks fine on the starboard bow!" he heard Quail yell. His heart missed a beat.

"Hard aport."

Waves broke menacingly against a black jagged pillar as the *Maid of Jeddore* swung away from its embrace.

"Steady," Haylestone ordered. As the great stone slid by he gave the helmsman a new course: "Steer nor'-east-by-north, Elmer." The hydrographic picture was in his head; he needed no chart to find his way. He knew he had just passed the Peg and Splinters.

They passed two more half-tide rocks close to starboard; then the loom of high land suddenly appeared almost ahead. In four strides Haylestone reached the telegraph and swung the handle to "full astern."

As the way lessened amid a vibration which appeared to proclaim an attempt on McNiff's part to pull the thrashing screw off the end of the shaft, the steep cliffs rose before them – but there was a gap!

At slow speed and with only a slight alteration of course the *Maid of Jeddore*, piloted by a skilful master, passed through a cleft in the hills between Perdoo Promontory and Cork Island.

Inside, the harbour was so small that the misty shore could be faintly seen all round. With a muffled clanging the chain ran out of the hawse pipe and they lay quietly at anchor.

They waited until dusk had dissolved into night, until the lights of the hamlet of Port Perdoo three quarters of a mile away were glimmering hazily over the water. It was only then that Haylestone announced to Quail and McNiff in the bright little mess-room that he was satisfied to go.

"Inspector Pogson will be away up the coast by now. We'll haul well out to sea – give the coast a wide berth. Warm up below, will you Angus, and Merv will heave in the anchor in five minutes."

Angus McNiff went out.

Haylestone was in the act of lacing a final mug of tea with a liberal splash of Schreecher's Newfoundland rum when the chief almost fell in over the high galley door step adjoining the mess-room.

"Hiram. Another valve spring's gone!"

"What!" Haylestone almost rammed the bottle through the table as he lowered it.

"Spare-me-days!" breathed Quail with almost as fast perception.

The captain and chief engineer tried to talk it over but they both did so at once until they were shouting at each other's heads. McNiff claimed it was driving the engine so hard coming in, and the curse of the grisly gravestones down in the hold exercising their evil influence. Haylestone bellowed that he must clear the coast under cover of darkness and did not want to be seen by the fishermen of Port Perdoo in the morning.

Finally Quail, the man of action when least expected, handed each a full mug of neat Schreecher's and then poured himself one. Presently things seemed less strenuous and McNiff condescended to go below again.

At two o'clock in the morning, when the metallic sounds which had risen from the engine room had grown fewer, the fog cleared. This was reported to the captain together with the intelligence that the lights of a vessel could be seen out beyond Cork Island. Haylestone came out of his cabin with his binoculars and studied the lights.

"Blast it! I believe it's him, lurking there outside the Peg and Splinters." He handed the glasses to the mate to have a look. "He won't try to make the gap in darkness but come daylight he'll negotiate the rocks and channel all right. I suppose it was his fancy radar that followed us here. I must get one of those gadgets one day."

"That's the RCMP," Quail confirmed, handing back the glasses.

Haylestone went down and stood at the top of the engine room ladder. "We're bottled, Angus; bottled up," he called, looking down at the engine where McNiff was working. "Come up on deck."

A conference was held. It was a tense and desperate session; one devoid of recrimination in the face of the enemy. McNiff stated that he would be less than an hour now. Quail said he could do his part of the operation in about an hour but he would not commit himself too rigidly. But glad he'd be to do it.

McNiff went below again and Quail hurried along the fore deck. They opened up the hold, swung the derrick over and commenced hoisting out the contraband under dimmed lighting.

"Line 'em up against the bulwark on the starboard side," Haylestone ordered.

As the work progressed Haylestone paced the deck with bowed head. He was glad to place his back to the unprofitable operation at each turn of his pacing, yet he could not bring himself to forsake the fore deck. Periodically he was drawn to examining the stones leaning against the bulwark, bulbous base down, monuments fit for the best city cemetery, he reflected, let alone a country churchyard. He admired particularly the white ones trimmed with narrow black borders. The two-toned browns were not bad but rather dreary; the greys were much more elegant. Personally, if he were asked to choose – and he did not feel himself ready yet – he would select the pebbled black kind which sparkled in the small beam of his flashlight.

Wonderful stuff plastic! Very versatile. He noticed that some had partial inscriptions on them which was a pretty accommodating idea, he thought. The upper surface of several stones were dedicated "To the Memory of . . . " with faint ruled lines beneath like a government form. And he noticed a white stone which had a stanza chiselled on the lower quarter – or printed in some way:

Distressing as it is to die
Beneath this stone it's nice to lie.

Perhaps it was just a sample with a sales angle; a pamphlet was probably supplied providing selections of other suitable verse.

Indeed, Haylestone was very distressed at the grave loss he was voluntarily about to incur. Was it flotsam or jetsam? He could never remember which was which. Anyway, it would represent a sinking fund – two or three fathoms down. His heart was kept from breaking only by the urgent need to clear his account with the law.

When the special cargo was all up on deck Merv took soundings while the hatches were being replaced and the derrick lowered.

"Three fathoms," he reported.

"Tide's rising," muttered Haylestone. "Eighteen feet isn't bad if we dump them all in the same place. Should be easy to fish up by and by in three fathoms of water. You can start to heave the anchor up, Merv, while the hands pitch them over."

He went off to the bridge to take some compass bearings to fix the exact position and then get the vessel underway, McNiff having stated that the engine was in working order.

In fact, McNiff went so far, after fixing things below, as to lend a hand to discharge the cargo – an unheard of performance. He growled abuses at the heinous objects as he and the cook bent down, lifted and pitched and bent again. The seamen were doing the same thing with a *joie de vivre* that developed into a rhythmic system rather like a bucket brigade at a fire. They needed no lights now in spite of the dark night. They merely heard the splashes; that was good enough.

The *Maid of Jeddore* came boldly out to sea with her steaming lights burning bright and clear, slid by the moaning Peg and Splinters as if her captain had been running the reefs for years, and passed close under the lee of the Royal Canadian Mounted Police.

No immediate steps were taken by the "enemy" to intercept. Pogson was either resting or was taken by surprise by the audacious manoeuvre. But Haylestone noted that the police boat soon turned and followed in his wake. Shadowing he thought it was called. It reminded him of the twelve-mile limit in the days of prohibition.

Soon after dawn Inspector Pogson dispatched a boarding party who made a thorough search of the holds in spite of Haylestone's fitting protests about the police impeding the peaceful pursuit of trade on the high seas. He made it clear to the sergeant that he had taken refuge during the night merely to repair his engine.

After that the RCMP seemed to lose interest and Pogson veered off.

The *Maid of Jeddore* was lying at her Halifax wharf. The mate and the chief were leaning back on the mess-room settee resting after their heavy breakfast and listening to their captain rehearsing a speech for delivery to Mr. Brass when he arrived on board. Suddenly the cook came in and thrust The Halifax Mail-Star into the orator's hands.

"Look, Skipper! See what it says!"

He pointed to a fairly large headline in the right hand column of the front page.

"'GHOSTLY HAPPENINGS AT PORT PERDOO'", the captain read out. Then the pointed beard shot forward. "What! . . . What's this? Blow me down!"

Hiram Haylestone rattled the paper vertically before his eyes:

> Inhabitants of this fishing village are scared out of their wits at the sudden appearance of a graveyard on their rugged shore. In the early hours of Wednesday when the fishermen came down to their boats they were startled at the sight of a series of gravestones just beyond the lapping water of the beach. The monuments in the dawn light gave every appearance of being an ancient cemetery thrown up by some marine disturbance. Many stones were standing upright while some were leaning in a fashion not unusual in old burial grounds. Some were wreathed in seaweed though those near-

> est the shore looked surprisingly new in the half-light. The fishermen retired to their dwellings – their womenfolk would not go down to the shore – and shortly afterwards Ephraim Jason set out to find the minister of the church.

Haylestone threw down the paper. "Well, I'll be darned! Plastic doesn't sink!"

"Floats, obviously," McNiff observed.

Mervin Quail spoke through his pipe stem which he gripped tightly in his side teeth, "Floats! Well, spare-me-days, Hiram!'

They hardly noticed the knock on the door. Another rap and the door opened. A short, stout man stepped in.

"Ah! Captain Haylestone," he said genially, "The gent I want to see."

Haylestone momentarily felt as though he lacked oxygen. "Er . . . Why . . . It's Mr. Brass! Well, I was expecting you – then I wasn't."

"A few words alone, Captain, if you don't mind. Could the crowd here leave us for a few minutes?"

"Sure . . . Sure, Mr. Brass. Okay Mate, Chief."

The other occupants of the mess-room removed themselves quite quickly, Haylestone thought dimly.

"I see you've read the morning paper, Captain," Brass said, sitting down in the mate's chair.

"Those stupid bloody fishermen! And I thought you were going to see that the coast was clear, Mr. Brass. I had a hell of a manoeuvre to get out of that one. Who would ever expect stones to float?"

Brass held up a pudgy hand. "Just a minute, Captain. Just a minute. I'll come to the point." He leaned back and the chair swivelled a bit. "You didn't fulfill the charter – not fully – but you brought the shipment into Nova Scotia. I heard of this yesterday and had my agent in Bridgewater down to Port Perdoo right away. He has already rounded up the monuments. I've got them in my scrap yard now. So . . . I have to reduce your freightage." He spread his hands. "It was too high anyway. I'll cut it thirty per cent – plus the price of two pieces that went out to sea on the ebb tide."

"Rounded them up . . . In your scrap yard . . . Thirty? Thirty per cent did you say?"

"Thirty per cent."

Haylestone gazed out the porthole as though searching for the sun. "Near seventy per cent of original contract less two stones. Yeah. That ought to keep the rigging tight on the *Maid of Jeddore*." Then he pushed himself up out of his chair and spoke brightly. "Is it too early for a drop of Schreecher's, Mr. Brass?"

# Pandemonium in the Cockpit

The *Maid of Jeddore* had rounded Nantucket Shoals in the morning mist and had headed for Rhode Island Sound. By early afternoon she was still plodding along, her heavy mainsail steadying the swing and dip of her wooden hull. The September sun shone warmly through the haze; all was peace. The occasional warbling bleat of the coaster's deck cargo of sheep reached the ears of Captain Hiram Haylestone as he leaned against the rail on the lee side of the bridge.

"Good to be back in the livestock trade," he remarked to the mate beside him for about the fifth time since leaving Canadian waters.

Mervin Quail pulled on his pipe but did not answer. He seldom did. The top of his bulky pants, supported by wide suspenders, polished the rail in front of him as it slid across his belly with each roll. He did not pay much attention to the sheep but he had expressed a liking for the bull that was tethered to a ring-bolt on the port side of the fore deck.

"Not much weight in animals," Captain Haylestone added.

He had picked up a consignment of pedigree stock in Prince Edward Island for a ranch in Connecticut. From New Haven he was going on to New York with the Newfoundland lobsters which were stowed in the holds of the little trader. Freight rates were high for both.

The captain went to the port side of the bridge and looked to windward. "Sou'-sou'-west. Proper fog wind," he remarked when he returned. He threw the stump of his cigar over the side. "I'm going to lie down – going to put an even strain on all parts while I can. Likely be real thick up around Block Island. Let's know if it shuts in."

Captain Haylestone went to his cabin leading off the wheel-house, kicked off his heavy boots and lay down on his bunk, a hard bed which he had lengthened to seven feet when he had first bought the vessel.

He seemed hardly to have dropped off when Mervin Quail was at his door. "Fog," he said laconically.

They stood together again. The fog banks rolled by in dense layers.

"Better blow the horn a bit, Merv, though the livestock won't like it."

Merv Quail stepped into the wheel-house, reached up and pulled the cord. A blast came from the air horn above. The sheep crouched in their pens.

When the sound died away the plunk of the diesel resumed, and the swish of the bow wave, like the slow scything of grass, returned. The scarred yellow foremast swung only perceptibly now before the vapour that hung down to the sea in a narrow semicircle.

Then they heard a more distant sound.

"Fog horn yonder," Quail muttered, nodding to starboard.

Haylestone stretched his long neck forward and turned his dark, bearded face in the direction of the warning notes. "Two or three fog horns it seems like . . . Slow speed," he called to the man at the wheel. The bell of the engine room telegraph made a grinding clank.

Mervin Quail went to the weather side and stood listening. As they moved slowly forward there seemed to be a general hubbub of hooting but it was more to leeward.

"A bunch of boats in a regatta caught in the fog, I expect," Haylestone soliloquized. "Dang fools. Wasting their time out on the water when they could be enjoying the fleshpots ashore. Don't know when they're well off. If I . . . "

Quail was shouting. "Vessel coming up to port!"

Almost instantly there was a crash and a rending sound of splitting timber. A violent shock ran through the boat. The bridge personnel tottered. The diffused light of the damp sun was abruptly obscured.

Regaining his equilibrium Haylestone leapt through the wheel-house to the weather side. A dark cloud was descending. Glancing up he saw an enormous blue sail, undulating like an octopus, crowding in on him and threatening to envelop the whole of the upperworks. He caught sight of a slender swaying mast reaching fifty feet above him.

"Stop engines!" he shouted over his shoulder to the helmsman.

Below him was a long slim yacht. She had struck, end on, just ahead of the bridge structure. She had come out of the fog bank full tilt with the wind behind her, her vast spinnaker billowing high and far before her. Her sharp white bow had pierced the bulwark at the deck and was wedged between a pair of stout mooring bits.

There was pandemonium in the cockpit. Orders were hurled from aft at the men leaping forward. The yacht's huge mainsail was coming down in the water under her out-reaching boom. Sheets and halyards were tangling.

Down on deck Merv Quail was yelling for his men. White-sweatered, yellow-trousered yachtsmen were jumping aboard. All hands tried to push the yacht's bow back through the gash in the bulwark.

The skipper, recognizable by his dark glasses and yachting cap, leaped out of his cockpit, rushed forward, looked, pushed, then dashed back.

"Get a sledge hammer, jacks, axes, saw," Haylestone directed from above. A man ran off.

But the *Maid of Jeddore* still had some headway and the yacht's stem was jamming tighter between the sturdy wooden mooring posts.

"Half astern," Haylestone called back to the wheel-house.

Above the tumult orders rang out on the yacht. "Cut the spinnaker adrift – let it go . . . Winchmen, lay aft and keep the bow up . . . Belay the forestay! . . . Hit it! Don't play with it . . . " The racing skipper stamped around his cockpit. "Hit it! Heave ho! . . . Push, you fools!"

He redirected his bellowing. "What's the matter with your damn ship? Can't you back off?"

Haylestone's voice transcended the hollering and hammering: "Can't move sideways, you idiot. I'm working you out with my engines as it is . . . Let her have it, Merv. Use two sledges . . . Stop engines," he called to the wheel-house. Then back to his opponent, "What's your name? Where do you hail from?"

But Haylestone could not wait for the reply – not that he got one. "Mind that bloody bull! He's adrift! Lookout below! Who cut the bull out? . . . Slow ahead."

The carpenters at the bulwark scattered as though Haylestone were drawing a bead with his bear gun. The bull moved menacingly down the deck dragging its halter from the ring in its nose.

"What are you doing there?" yelled the undiscerning skipper from the cockpit. "Don't waste time!"

"Spare-me-days!" shouted Quail. "Grab him. And keep that spinnaker from flapping or the bull will charge."

The brown and white monster, low slung in the bilges, swung his head from side to side, then gradually lowered it.

Haylestone yelled down that if he got foul of the ladder he'd break his horns. "That's a prize bull. Prize cargo!"

The cook made a dive for the dragging halter but the snorting bull lunged at him before he could reach it. Two of the yacht's crew fell over the side onto their own craft which brought blasts from their skipper. Quail tried to lasso the animal with a running bowline but it tangled with its horns and seemed to irritate it.

Elmer had got between the bull and the rail, like a good seaman. He grabbed a fold of the spinnaker and with the skill of a toreador threw the blue sail over the beast's head. The cook had another go and this time caught the halter.

"Hitch that other rope on," Quail sang out and leapt into the fray. "That's it. Take a turn round the rigging."

"All heave away now," Haylestone ordered from above. "Don't hurt him! . . . That's right. Moor him to the rigging."

"Boat's coming!" shouted a man with an axe who had resumed his place at the scene of the crash. "All aboard!"

The yacht's crew jumped over the splintered bulwark. The *Maid of Jeddore* was gathering way again and the yacht's bow was cracking. Then she unplugged like a stopper from a bottle.

"Keep her off . . . Boathooks . . . Stand by the mainsail." The young crewmen danced furiously in their yellow oilskins to the tune of their skipper's commands from the cockpit.

"What's your name, damn you?" Haylestone thundered again from aloft. "Where're you from?"

But the yacht slithered down the side like a barge being poled off a mud-hopper. He made no impression. No one answered. No one saw him any more. Looking back at her jagged jutting bow Haylestone was reminded of a crocodile with its mouth open.

No sooner was she free than her mainsail was hoisted and her enormous jib went up. She was off on the course she came in on. But she had parted with her spinnaker. That massive cloud of sailing perfection was spread over the *Maid's* boat deck and lay in heaps on the deck aft.

A rope thrashing about struck Haylestone. The vast blue spinnaker was flapping over the wheelhouse and had fouled in the after rigging.

Haylestone told Ambrose to ring down "stop." "We'll collect ourselves," he murmured, half to himself. He called down to the fore deck, "When you've belayed the bull to the ringbolt, Merv, furl this blasted spinnaker. It'll be afire on the funnel in a minute. Who the hell cut the bull adrift?"

A voice came from behind him: "I guess I did." A yachtsman suddenly appeared like a phantom. Haylestone threw up his arms.

"You . . . You cut the bull adrift!" he roared. "Thought you'd all gone."

"She's gone without me," spluttered the leftover visitor, pointing a palsied finger at the departing boat. "She veered off before I could get back aboard. You the skipper?"

"What do I look like – the cook?" Haylestone barked. "You mean you cut . . . "

"I've got to get back to the yacht, Skipper." He spoke fast. "Will you put all steam on and catch her for me before she gets to the finish line? She's steering nor'-nor'-east."

"This isn't a steamboat; she's diesel."

"You can overtake her if you go after her now, surely. She still has two miles to run. I must get back."

The young man was the athletic type and was demonstrating it by hopping from one rubber-soled shoe to the other while agitatedly watching the disappearing stern view of the fast- sailing yacht.

"Overtake her with all this corruption aboard?" Haylestone rejoined, thrusting an arm out in the direction of the rippling mass of blue. "Are you responsible for all this? And my bust bulwark?"

"I helped to cut the spinnaker away," explained the man in the glistening yellow pants. He spoke passionately.

"And the bull?"

"Maybe. I was slashing about with my knife. Can you get me back aboard, Skipper?"

"No," said Haylestone. He suddenly felt sorry for the fellow. He had no idea that a man, piddling around in a yacht, could be so ardent. "They can finish without you."

Love shone from the yachtsman's eyes as he gazed nostalgically at the billowing blue fabric being taken in by the men. "They can't," he murmured.

The fog had partially lifted. Haylestone now saw a great array of boats to leeward and ahead of him. There were hundreds of them: sailing boats, big power cruisers, even ferries, and he could recognize some coast guard vessels by their red-banded white hulls.

"See that, Skipper?" The young man was pointing to another yacht similar to his own coming out of the mist to windward. He clasped his hands tightly. "That's the challenger.'

"She can't catch your boat," Haylestone observed.

"No. We're coming up to the buoy." He spoke as though he was still aboard his yacht.

Boats were clustered along what appeared to be the finish line, leaving a path for the racers. Then a blare of hooting broke out from the spectator fleet.

"She's over the line," muttered the yachtsman. "But she's got a flag up. Protest flag, I'll bet."

Then his blond head fell. "What's the use?" he whispered, and went slowly down the ladder as though his canvas shoes were soled with lead. Haylestone noticed him talking to the sheep on the fore deck.

Ambrose turned the big wheel. "Didn't get an answering ring on the telegraph when I signalled to stop her, Skipper."

"What!" Haylestone, now in the wheel-house, gave the handle several swings that shook the pedestal to its bolts. There was no answer. He went out and looked at the water. She was still making way. Coming back he blew down the engine room voice pipe and listened.

"Angus," he shouted. He blew again, long and hard, but there was no answer.

In the meantime the mate had been directing the deck hands in the task of disengaging the spinnaker that enshrouded two-thirds of the vessel, an undulating sea of blue. In the process they uncovered the chief engineer.

They found Angus McNiff flat out on the after deck and when the men leapt forward, throwing the sail cloth aside, and lifted him, they found his round form as inert as a corpse. Haylestone rushed to the scene leaving Ambrose in charge of the bridge.

"Quick, Skipper, he looks dead," begged the second engineer who had been helping to clear the decks when they unearthed what appeared to be the remains of his chief.

"They've pulled the plug on him proper by the looks of it," someone speculated.

The cook put his ear to McNiff's hairy chest. "It's ticking," he announced, and ran off to the galley for water. Haylestone pulled off his cap and listened, then examined his almost bald head. He turned him over gently, calling for artificial respiration.

Merv Quail knew about restoring drowning men. He straddled McNiff's back and started to work on his ribs. The cook sloshed cold water over his head and neck. The second engineer stood by wringing his hands. Haylestone caught him by the back of his shirt collar and told him to get below. "Engine's unattended. She's going ahead. Stop her."

McNiff vomited and moved slightly. Perhaps it was the mention of his engine.

"I know!" exclaimed the cook. "It's as . . . aspyxia. That ruddy sail covered the funnel and engine room ventilators and the fumes came back down the casing into the engine room. I felt it in the galley. Poor old Angus . . . been aspyxiated. More water." He poured liberally from his bucket.

They concluded that the chief must have felt ill – carbon monoxide – and had struggled up the engine room ladder to get some fresh air and collapsed by the after winch.

They all had a very alarming ten minutes until Angus McNiff raised himself on his elbow and said he must pump the bilges. By this time Ambrose had recalled the captain to the bridge with a series of short blasts on the fog horn, and Haylestone arrived in time to see a coast guard boat bearing down. She swung round and drew alongside.

"Were you in collision with *Scimitar*, Cap?"

Haylestone stood in the wing of his little bridge with his legs apart and his hands clasped behind his back. "Who's *Scimitar*?" He did not use his full vocal power in spite of the throbbing honk of the coast guard's engine.

"You don't know! . . . don't know *Scimitar*! She just came around the buoy damaged. Said she'd been in collision with a boat on the leeward leg of the race."

"Sailboat rammed my vessel."

"Sailboat rammed you!" The man ducked inside his wheel-house and Haylestone saw him grab a telephone off the bulkhead. Then he found the errant yachtsman standing beside him.

"You must be a stranger in American waters, Skipper. This was the America's Cup Race and today's race was the seventh and final one of the series. And we were leading – *Scimitar*, the yacht that hit you." His voice faltered and, shading his eyes, he looked towards the throng of craft moving away from the marker buoy, including the two tall sails of the racers.

The coast guard skipper swung out on deck and looked up. "You've had it, Cap!"

Haylestone did not catch his next statement because it was interrupted by the cook who wanted to report that they had Angus in his bunk, but he seemed in a low condition.

"That's carbon monoxide all right," said Haylestone seriously. "Better get him into hospital quick, I guess."

"That's what I was thinking," agreed the cook.

The captain thought a moment. "We'll go into Newport. Too dangerous to wait till we get to New Haven."

"Good." The cook, like all cooks, knew just where they were. "The men'll be glad to hear it. They're worried." He retired backwards down the ladder and Haylestone went into the wheel-house. He rang full speed and told the helmsman to steer north-by-west. He pulled the cord above him and a blast from the air horn warned the coast guard boat he was turning to starboard.

It was nearly five o'clock when the *Maid of Jeddore* dropped anchor among the high-priced yachts and cruisers in Newport Harbour. Haylestone had asked by radio for a doctor and the Newport medical launch was there to meet them. The cook and an orderly helped the chief across the deck and over the gangplank. The doctor had ordered him to hospital. McNiff looked very pale; he did not speak and seemed mesmerized as he was borne to the launch. Haylestone himself carried his grip which the cook had hurriedly packed. Some of the crew had their caps in their hands and all talked in low voices when they spoke. As the launch left someone said it was as if the *Maid of Jeddore* had been dismasted.

Suddenly a speed boat, enveloped in spray, was seen approaching. It skidded alongside like a skier doing a stop christie. A yachting character leapt from it and asked for the skipper. Haylestone was just going into the mess-room to revive himself with a mug of coffee.

"Compliments of the chairman of the race committee," the yachting type conveyed breathlessly.

"Would you be kind enough to repair on board the committee boat at the pier near Brenton Cove for a few words with him – right away if you can."

"What does he want with me? Who is he?"

"Jefferson Trott. He's the final authority on the races. Its urgent, Skipper. Very urgent."

"Oh." Haylestone turned and surveyed the livestock on the fore deck. He felt as depressed as the sheep appeared to be. Cost of delay with perishable lobsters in the hold was one thing but the danger of poor old Angus foundering was quite another. To see him intoxicated from unnatural causes was very worrying.

"I'll take you in my boat, Skipper," the young man was saying. "There's no time to lose if you don't mind."

"Where's the captain of that blasted sailboat that rammed my vessel?"

"He's on board the committee boat with Jefferson Trott."

"That's the man I want to see," Haylestone snarled through clenched teeth, grasping the air with his huge hands as though he was strangling a limp figure. The yachting character winced.

Haylestone marched aft; the young man followed.

He told Merv Quail he wanted him to go with him to support his evidence. The unfortunate afternoon passenger was very anxious to go too. They wound through the traffic towards the pier at a high, roaring speed, greatly to Quail's disgust.

They could not help marvelling at the symmetry of the two 12-metre yachts berthed at the boatyard as they passed, in spite of the terrible gash in the bow of the one under the stars and stripes. The other one, Haylestone noticed, wore the white ensign.

Aboard the committee boat they were hastily piloted below, down a little carpeted stairway into a sumptuous saloon. Several sporting types were deployed around the table. A large, florid greyhaired man rose to greet Haylestone and Quail.

"You the skipper of that sheep boat?" He could hardly fail to recognize the master of a coaster; the tarnished gold on his cap and salt-impregnated jacket were universal. Tall and swarthy, he was hard to mistake. "I'm Jefferson Trott. Responsible for conduct of races. You are . . . ?"

"Captain Hiram Haylestone."

"Good. These gentlemen help me in my decisions." He swept his hand around.

"Where's the skipper of the boat that rammed the *Maid of Jeddore*?"

"Ah, yes." Jefferson Trott glanced at a square, hard-looking outdoorsman sitting at the table. "This is Mr. Edson Featherstonehaugh Pyle III."

Haylestone said he was glad at last to know what he called himself and that he realized now there had been no time to disclose all that when he had been clinched to his bulwark like a barnacle.

"Please sit down," Mr. Jefferson Trott ordered, taking up a standing position himself at the end of the table and thrusting his hands, thumbs protruding, into the pockets of his blue and gold blazer which was cut to under-emphasize his proportions. "I'll come to the point – we have little time, the press is waiting for us."

He launched into an oration that in tone was a cross between an address before a naval court martial and a speech at a sod-turning ceremony at a penitentiary. After pointing out the great significance of the international race, he said that the committee had to resolve a protest of one of the contenders before meeting the press, a powerful body, and in order to resolve it they needed Captain Haylestone's cooperation. The facts were that his cattle boat had got in *Scimitar's* way, had been across the course line, had not avoided her, and the committee felt justified in validating *Scimitar's* protest that the yacht had been subjected to an unnatural, unfair, and wholly unexpected hazard, and under conditions where the visibility was reduced to a mere boat's length. "The race committee want you, in fact expect you, in view of the momentous meaning of the occasion, to accept responsibility for the accident."

Captain Hiram Haylestone had been gripping the red leather arms of his chair and was slowly lifting himself as Jefferson Trott concluded his thesis.

"I will not! Unnatural hazard by damn! Me? . . . across his course line!" He was standing, leaning forward, his hands flat on the polished table. "I got in the way?" His forehead was flushed – it was the only part of his dark hairy face that could betray his blood pressure. "What the hell's all this malarky? Whose waters . . . "

Trott held up his hand. "Captain Hornblower . . . "

"Haylestone! Haylestone! Do you hear me? And, furthermore," he hit the table with his massive fist and the ash trays jumped, "whose waters are these? Yours for the exclusive use of racing your sailboats? Now let me tell you . . . "

"Please, Skipper . . . "

"Captain! I'm not the skipper of a sailboat!"

"Yacht."

"Okay. Yacht. Now," he looked down at Edson Featherstonehaugh Pyle III, whose broad shoulders seemed to have contracted under the weight of international responsibility, "I was going slow. You were going all out – full-and-by. I was blowing my horn. I didn't hear yours. You were on an overtaking course, not crossing; therefore I didn't have to keep out of your way. You were at fault, Mister."

"Where's your chart?"

"Don't use charts."

"Don't use charts?"

"Don't use charts. The coast's in my head."

"Did you see the collision occur?" asked Pyle III, leaning forward in his chair and pulling at his turtleneck with a finger.

"No. My mate did though. I was blinded by your bloody spinnaker."

"And what did he see?" demanded one of the committeemen promptly, before Pyle III could get the question in.

Quail was filling his pipe under the table.

"What did you see, Merv?" Haylestone repeated kindly.

Silence fell for a moment, then Merv said, "Collision."

"From what direction?"

"Abaft the beam."

"Overtaking!" Haylestone concluded and sat down slowly. He pulled a White Owl from an inner pocket. A neighbouring committeeman reached for the box of cigars on the table and pushed them towards him. Haylestone lit his own.

"You know the race was the most important event of its kind in the world, don't you?" the committeeman shot at him.

"Can't be. Never heard of it before."

"What! The America's Cup?"

A man across the table said the captain would tell them next he had never heard of the New York Yacht Club.

"Heard of the New York Temperance Club," Haylestone answered. "That outfit got in my way once or twice."

A lull came again like the calm at the centre of a cyclone. Merv Quail took his pipe out of his mouth. "Maybe this gent," he rumbled slowly, jerking his thumb at Pyle III, "mistook the *Maid of Jeddore's* sail for the other feller he was racing against."

It was as though a starting gun had been fired under the saloon table.

All the committee seemed to have a go at Quail. Then Jefferson Trott came in.

"This won't do, gentlemen," he announced loudly. "The press. We can't keep them waiting much longer." He looked impatiently around at his yachting fellows on either side of him. "We must accede to *Scimitar's* protest. She must be exonerated."

They all endorsed the concept.

"You see, Captain," Trott went on, mopping his flushed face with a handkerchief, "it's the public. We've got to shift the blame from *Scimitar.*"

"What does it matter; she won, didn't she?" Haylestone was incredulous.

"She didn't. That's the point. She looked as if she did; the spectators think she did. They'll be drinking to her success all through the fleet by now. But technically she didn't. That's the tragedy. There was a certain handicap. And the Great American Public will soon know the truth. But we've got to coat the pill. We need you . . . your co-operation, Captain Hayleblower."

"stone!"

"stone. To be frank, we want *you* to take the blame; that is, for the collision . . . "

"Me take the blame! For the sake of the Great American Public! When the captain here split my bulwark and sent my chief engineer to hospital?" Glaring at Edson Featherstonehaugh Pyle III, he tried to pound into his crewcut head what his spinnaker had done to McNiff and its probable influence on his life. "And I came here to lodge a protest; to tell you what you're liable for." Turning towards the end of the table he jabbed the air above his head with his cigar as though preparing to hurl a belaying pin at the chairman. "And if you don't take it from me you'll take it from the marine insurance . . . or the courts." Having made the pronouncement he had wanted to get round to he rammed his White Owl back between his molars.

Jefferson Trott canted forward, hands outstretched. "I'm sorry, Skipper . . . Captain, I didn't make myself clear. The New York Yacht Club will pay the cost of repairs and the medical expenses of your engineer. Very sorry about that. All we want you to do is to accept responsibility for the collision – you know: 'it was all my fault for being where I was.' Tell the press that when they ask you. And there's no need to think of your insurance company. The race committee will see to it that you are completely recompensed."

Haylestone crouched, putting his hands on the edge of the table as though he were going to push it across the saloon. "All hospital expenses for Chief Engineer McNiff," he began to enumerate. "His convalescence and transportation to rejoin the vessel. There will be $500 for cutting the bull adrift and endangering the crew thereby; $1,000 a day for delaying my vessel on passage; fifteen per cent of the freight on the lobsters because that proportion will be dead by the time I get to New York – and compensation for my reputation for live delivery. And of course the bulwark – quite a repair job."

"You can take it from Jefferson Trott," the chairman said, rising and glancing at the door, "that the Club will pay. You got in the way, Captain, and couldn't avoid the yacht, okay?"

Captain Haylestone nodded. Trott told him to call at the Yacht Club in New York when he got there and present his expenses. "And now for the announcement and the business of meeting the press," he said to the others.

Three days later the *Maid of Jeddore* was in New York discharging her lobsters.

Haylestone was called to the telephone at the agent's office on the fish wharf.

"Hiram!" said a voice. "Hiram!"

"Angus!"

"Pipe down, Hiram. You're not talking down your voice pipe now."

"Where are you, Angus? You all right?"

"Sure. All parts turning over like I was running on New York's best American lube oil. All okay aboard?"

"You bet. Cripes! I'm glad to hear your voice."

"First time I ever heard that. You're invited to pick me up at the N.Y.Y.C."

"What tavern's that?"

"New York Yacht Club on West Forty-Fourth. Ask the hall porter for Mr. McNiff. I'll probably be sitting under one of them glittering chandeliers at the main bar. Bring Merv up too. Drinks are on the house, Hiram."

The porter was certainly acquainted with Mr. McNiff. Passing through lofty pictured halls they found him at a long bar.

"They did me handsome at the hospital. Shipped me here by private plane. Never been in a club before. Splendid accommodation. But I'm not much favoured by the inmates."

"None of us are anywhere."

The liveried barman regretted he had not heard of Schreecher's Newfoundland Rum but thought he could provide a good substitute. Haylestone moved along sideways to admire the tiers of bottles and display of crystal.

"What really happened, Merv? I've only had what the papers said and I don't believe them." Angus McNiff looked through his down-growing eyebrows which partially screened his vision.

"Spare-me-days! It was a funny business," Merv answered slowly. "Fair stuff this," he murmured, looking into his glass.

"Well?"

"The Americans won . . . but they didn't."

"So it seemed. But the *Maid of Jeddore* is as popular as a sullage scow. Took a terrible beating in the papers."

"You explain it, Hiram," Merv said as Haylestone rejoined.

"Well, they wanted a deal and I made it. Profitable too, Angus. But when we got to New Haven we found we were the object of all kinds of blasphemy. You see, the American boat crossed the finish line first in spite of her accident – and it was the final race of the series – but she was disqualified because there was a rule which said that a yacht must finish with the same number of men on board that she had when she started. And we had that guy *Scimitar* left behind. So she lost the race. But it eased Pyle the third's public image to blame me. Mind you, Angus, I wasn't at fault and don't you think so for a moment. Merv can prove that."

"Well!" exclaimed Angus McNiff, and they all drank.

When he had ordered another round, McNiff said he was going to take them to the Model Room and show them the America's Cup.

"It's fastened to the centre of the table and you should see the bolt underneath. It's unique – a trick bolt. And the spanner's kept in the vault. I'd like to be here when they unscrew that bolt."

# Loading Deep

Two lobster boats lay alongside the *Maid of Jeddore.* From the dock their dark images against the black hull of the coastal freighter could not easily be seen in the November evening drizzle – the pools of light from the two lamps on the wharf fell on the still water too close to the dock wall.

Captain Haylestone was encouraging with stunning outbursts several members of his crew in their task of carrying sacks of potatoes across the fore deck to the off-shore side and passing them down over the rail to the lobstermen. It was an unusual procedure. An uninformed onlooker would have been justified in questioning why the cargo was not being lowered into the open hold, still only four-fifths full.

It was eleven o'clock when their thumping engines had driven the lobstermen down the misty blackness of Halifax Harbour. The *Maid of Jeddore's* hatches were battened down but she did not sail until eight in the morning, after the deputy port warden had been down to clear the vessel for sea.

Captain Hiram Haylestone watched the port official on the wharf examining the newly-painted white load-line marks on the hull in the pale morning light. He saw him look along the vessel's wooden side and up at the mast.

Haylestone shifted his cigar and muttered to the chief engineer out of the corner of his mouth that he knew the damned crank would do that. "He's as suspicious as a sea lawyer."

"Ain't without some reason, I'd say," the chief retorted.

"You've got an off-shore list, Capt'n," the deputy port warden called across, "and your winter marks are on the water's edge. If she was on an even keel they would be down out of sight."

"Come aboard." The captain's voice echoed along Water Street.

Haylestone showed him several tons of gash on the starboard side of the upper deck, old dunnage and rubbish brought up from the holds after cleaning, which he said they were going to dump when they got out to sea, and the chief engineer added that the bilges were full of oil which could not be pumped out in the dock, of course. The captain testified this would lighten and straighten the vessel and the winter marks would be well clear of the water.

The deputy port warden finally selected a document from the files of an inner pocket and handed it over in rather the same way as a bookie would pass over the winnings on a long odds race. But he had one more look at the white marks as he went ashore.

"She looks more seaworthy with load lines on her," he called up to the captain who had climbed the ladder to the bridge.

Captain Haylestone answered with three penetrating blasts on his air horn; and the little trader backed out. Black smoke and soot rose from her slim funnel.

Before noon she had made her rendezvous with the two lobster boats twenty miles to seaward of Sambro Island Lighthouse, just inside the eighty fathom line. Although there was a fair movement on the sea and the small boats bumped frequently against the *Maid of Jeddore*, the sacks were hoisted out and, without loss of potatoes, stowed down the holds quickly. When all was loaded there was hardly space in the hatchways to stow the slings and tackle.

"Good tight fit," Hiram Haylestone remarked as he went to the side and handed each boat owner his reward. "How's my marks now, Joe," he asked the fisherman in the round woollen cap.

"Well down out of sight, even when she rolls up."

"Thanks boys. Good lobstering."

He swung his vessel away when the boats had chugged clear and headed south towards the West Indies.

After dinner the captain and chief engineer sat on at the table. The cook refilled their coffee mugs.

"That's one way of doing it," Haylestone remarked happily.

"As you've already said," Angus McNiff responded. "But I don't like it, Hiram."

"We'll use this scheme until it wears out, then turn to other tactics when those lousy, interfering buzzards gain confidence in my conforming to the regulations."

Angus McNiff choked in his mug. He coughed several times, then said that the Nova Scotia winter would be like a tropical summer before that happened.

"Well, you never know."

But McNiff had accepted the stratagem the captain had adopted, grudgingly of course, because Haylestone had explained the economic necessity for it and he knew that Angus was aware, after all these years, of the problems that beset the master and owner of a vessel trying to make a margin of profit in the face of the perils of the sea, the Department of Transport, officials of ports, and occasionally the officers of the law. The immediate problem was to enable the *Maid of Jeddore* to continue to operate under the new amendment to the Canada Shipping Act.

In effect, this amendment meant that vessels of as little as 150 tons were to be subject to the load line rules and have painted on their sides Plimsoll marks similar to those of big ships.

But the *Maid of Jeddore* was only 149 tons. She

was free of this regulation and could continue to load down to her scuppers, which was what Captain Hiram Haylestone quite often did when he had a heavy cargo. It had been because of this very practice and the casualties it had caused, and the cost to Lloyd's, that the government amendment had been introduced. All would still have been satisfactory to Haylestone had the Department of Transport not decided to verify the gross tonnage of vessels close to the deadline.

The surveyor who came aboard the *Maid of Jeddore* had encountered resistance but he managed to take many internal measurements which, when worked out, revealed the vessel to be 158 tons. There must have been some mistake at one time, the surveyor suggested, because Haylestone had been getting away with murder for a long time, which he said his department had suspected.

It had been a terrible blow. But Hiram Haylestone had somehow survived it.

Now, in the comfort of the mess-room with the chief at the other end of the table, the captain was at peace; he was out at sea getting farther away every minute from the Minister of Transport.

McNiff scrutinized his cigarette as though it were a bolt with a stripped thread. "If you bring a deep cargo north what'll your plot be? It ain't the deep loading I care about, the *Maid* can take that, but if the DOT catches you it's the clink for you, Hiram, not just a fine. And where'll we be then?"

"You leave it to me, Angus. You haven't seen me short of ideas, have you?"

The *Maid of Jeddore* reached The Caribee, as Haylestone called the region, in nine days. They passed between Anguilla and the Virgin Islands in warm brilliant weather, which reminded them of their sailing days out of St. Thomas, and stood on towards St. Lucia. The encircling tropical hills cast their reflections deep across the almost tideless harbour of Port Castries as the *Maid* glided towards the shimmering town.

As the sweating natives gathered on the wharf to receive the cargo, the harbour master came aboard. He dropped his white sun helmet onto Haylestone's bunk.

"You didn't have marks on your sides the last time you were here, Capt'n."

"Didn't I?" Haylestone pulled a cork. "I knew I'd see you as soon as we came alongside, so I had the glasses polished up specially." He poured a liberal noggin into each. "Much trade these days?" he enquired.

"Fair. What's your draft?"

"Cheers," said Haylestone.

"Cheers. Good to see you back in Castries."

"Ah. I like this place."

"Your draft, Capt'n?"

"Blast these mosquitos! Where's that swatter?" Haylestone, who had not sat down yet, found the weapon and made a sortie.

"Mosquitos plentiful just now. Rainy season coming on," the harbour master explained. "Have you entered the draft in your log?"

"You know, I've been thinking," said Haylestone, gazing out of the porthole, glass in hand, "I'd like to have a drive around the island one day. Never seen it inland."

"Haven't you. Why, I might take you myself. About the draft now. How many feet is your vessel drawing?"

"Haven't looked at it yet. That would be good, a drive into the interior. Thanks very much."

"Since when did they stick those marks on? Matter of fact, if the water wasn't so clear here I wouldn't have noticed them beneath the surface."

"When? Well now . . . " Haylestone uncorked the bottle again with care and concentration. "Not bad stuff this Canadian rye, is it? I knew you liked it. Didn't have to ask you."

The harbour master held out his glass saying it was very good and watched the pale amber liquid rise until it reached the waist of the engraved mermaid.

"Always like to partly submerge her," said Haylestone.

"Like your Plimsoll mark."

Haylestone laughed boisterously. Then he was suddenly reminded of something. He excused himself and dug down into the bottom of his wardrobe at the foot of the bunk, pulling out hard-weather clothing and a pair of seaboots and eventually a bottle wrapped in canvas.

"I nearly forgot," he said, unwrapping it slowly and holding it up with the label towards the harbour master. "Canadian Club. Thought you'd like a bottle. When I found I was coming to St. Lucia I said to myself I'll get a bottle of rye for my old friend the harbour master."

"Well, that was a mighty good thought. Thank you indeed, Capt'n."

"I must tell you what happened when I was getting it." Haylestone had a long and involved story about how he went into a barber shop to have his hair and whiskers trimmed after he had been to the liquor store, and how the bottle was missing when he got out of the chair.

It was such a long account, embellished with details which even included a seagull that had stained his shore-going hat – must have been drinking acid, he thought – that three more drinks had been served, all up to the mermaid's bosom, before Haylestone considered it timely to take the harbour master ashore and walk him to his car.

When they had discharged the entire cargo, and after Haylestone had had a boring drive down the western side of the island with the harbour master and his wife, they left St. Lucia and pushed on to Barbados.

He was pleased to find that his cargo was ready for him in a shed at the Careenage. The Careenage had the advantage of being a dock with a depth of water of only fourteen and a half feet which was not enough to fully load the *Maid.*

They loaded sugar and barrels of molasses and kegs of rum and had to move out when the keel was a foot from the bottom. At anchor in Carlisle Bay they took from lighters the rest of the cargo that Haylestone had arranged for. She was bung full when they finished, and there was such a pleasant roll to the vessel in the swell that was coming into the bay that no one could tell whether the symbols of the Department of Transport were above water or below. Laden with fuel for the voyage home, the freeboard between the water and the deck was so slim that the sea occasionally came in through the freeing ports – the upper deck was almost awash.

They sailed from Barbados with what Hiram Haylestone believed the navy would refer to as "all dispatch." No use hanging around when you are loaded.

Two days later the *Maid of Jeddore* was lying inert in the Sargasso Sea. Now and then the heavy mainsail slatted as she swayed into the trade wind. Captain Haylestone was sitting on the collapsible stool in the shade of the wheel-house frowning at the miles of greenish-brown gulfweed floating on the water. It was the second time they had had to stop because of the weed, which was unusual. The plant had clogged the intake. Down in the fetid engine room Angus McNiff and the second engineer were clawing at fathoms of the marine phenomenon and dragging it out of pipes and elbows and what the chief referred to as the sea chest.

Haylestone closed his eyes. It was very hot. His beard gradually sank to his hairy chest. Presently a voice came to him telling him something about a vessel in the offing. He rose, stretched, looked across the vast field of gulfweed and saw a three-masted ship several miles away. As he watched he noticed her alter course towards them.

He called down to the mate on the fore deck, who was fishing for eels in the weed, to come up. Mervin Quail passed his line to one of the men and joined the captain.

"What's she bearing down on us for?" Haylestone wondered.

"Maybe she sees we're stopped and wants to offer assistance."

The stranger was now only a mile or so off.

"Better hoist the ensign, Merv."

"Ed," Merv Quail called down to the man with the fishing line. "Hoist the ensign. You'll find it in the rack over the galley stove. Left it there when it got wet."

"What the hell is Angus doing down below?" Haylestone growled. "He ought to have that stinking grass out by now." He went to the engine room voice pipe, pulled the cap off and blew down it.

"Angus, haven't you cleared your blasted intake yet? What are you doing, picking raspberries off the stuff?"

A thin sound came up.

"All right. All right," Haylestone responded. "But there's a fleet of ships bearing down on us and I don't want to look like we're stuck in the undergrowth."

The approaching vessel was stopping. She swung off about two hundred yards to windward and revealed her profile.

"Some ship!" Haylestone muttered.

Quail had nothing to add.

A lamp flashed from her bridge.

"That's funny," Haylestone remarked. "It's only navies and big ships that treat you to that stupid stuff. Can't be a Yankee millionaire. He'd telephone."

The usual disregard was preserved towards the morse code. Suddenly Quail noticed something.

"Spare-me-days, Hiram! You see her ensign. It's the white ensign."

"British Navy!"

They stood looking at the blue hull glittering in the sunshine, the tall tapering masts and the handsome yellow ochre funnel.

"I didn't know the British Navy hired drive-yourself craft," Quail offered.

Haylestone fetched his glasses. "*Britannia.* Well. Sounds British all right."

Then a voice through a megaphone came over the moss-covered sea.

"Do you require assistance?"

Haylestone cursed. He cupped his hands round his mouth. "No thank you." He would like to have added what he thought of McNiff.

The next enquiry was surprising.

"Have you an engineer on board who is familiar with American Worthington pumps?" The identity of the ship was confirmed by the English accent.

"Worthington pumps?" Haylestone rumbled. "Engineer?" He gazed mistily aft, the habit of all captains when thinking of engineers. "Why, I suppose so," he answered himself. "What of it?"

"He wants to know something from Angus," Merv Quail interpreted brightly.

"That's it." Haylestone swung round. "Aye aye, Capt'n. We've got him."

The clear English voice came back. "My engineer is having trouble with a new Worthington electric rotary pump he had installed in the Bahamas. If you will permit your engineer officer to come on board I shall send a boat."

"Angus aboard that hooker!" Quail exclaimed.

"Aye aye, Capt'n. Send your boat."

Haylestone had fully recovered. This was big business. Consultants to the Royal Navy! But he had undertaken to send Angus McNiff into a society somewhat above his station. And to involve him in a trip in an open boat! It would require all the captain's personal persuasion. He thudded down the ladder.

"Angus," Haylestone shouted down into the strangely silent cavern from the top step. "Forget that grass. Come up on deck. Quick. It's urgent. You've got to fix a pump that's baffled the admiralty experts."

McNiff pulled a long streamer out of the sea chest. "I'm picking bloody raspberries. You're blocking my light up there. Don't bother me. I told you that before when you yelled down the pipe."

Haylestone came down the oily ladder.

"Listen to me, Angus. There's a naval icebreaker or something lying off a cable to windward and her skipper says he's got engine trouble. His pump's broken down, Worthington rotary, and he wants a man who knows about Worthingtons to tell them how to fix it." He looked earnestly down into the chief engineer's round face, where impatience glowered through beads of sweat running between black smudges. "It's your big chance to serve the navy, Angus. Capt'n's sending a boat. You've got to go over and have a look at it."

"Me! Go aboard a vessel in mid-Atlantic . . . to fix a pump? You out of your mind, Hiram?" He seemed to stagger on the plates as though the vessel had taken a heavy lurch.

"They can't fix it. It's important to them. I promised you'd go."

Angus McNiff suddenly folded up like a telescope and collapsed onto a box upholstered with what had once been a DOT-approved lifebelt.

Haylestone reached down and took his sweaty arm. "Up, Angus, old friend. We'll get up on deck where there's some fresh air." He spoke like a hospital orderly.

He led the dazed chief to the foot of the ladder and pushed him up. On deck it was instantly apparent that the commander of the *Britannia* was a naval officer of action. A gleaming blue whaler was being rowed across the intervening distance as though all the sargasso in the Tropic of Cancer made no difference.

Haylestone took McNiff's arm again. "You see that vessel there, Angus, it's only a short pull. And you're going in that sturdy cutter, or whatever it is, rowed by Her Majesty's stalwarts. You'll be all right, Angus."

McNiff, naked to the waist except for a rag around his neck, his sagging pants making his legs look like those of a stunted zebra, hung on to the rail with both hands and stared through his down-growing eyebrows across the undulating gulfweed, past the small boat, to the blue ship.

"The royal yacht!" he breathed.

Haylestone jumped. "What! . . . Royal yacht! No! How do you know?"

"Royal yacht!" McNiff was sinking again. "Seen her at the opening of the Seaway, going up the Great Lakes. My heavens!"

Then, with the strength that comes to a hero in the face of high peril, he stood unsupported. "Worthington rotary . . . Give me a shirt someone," he commanded.

The cook was fortunately standing by to give a hand with the boat rope. He was the only one who ever wore a white shirt. He peeled it off and helped Angus into it like an overcoat. Angus McNiff did not take his eyes from the greatest vision in shipping as he tucked the shirt beneath his belt. The cook did up the buttons and wiped the chief's face with his apron.

"Want a lifebelt, Angus?" Haylestone asked.

"Lifebelt? No. If it's my last voyage, it's my last voyage. If you promised it, Hiram, I'll fulfil it." McNiff's voice had a gurgle in it like water running down a drain.

Haylestone laid a vast hand on Angus's shoulder. "You'll get a medal for this, you know, or one of those OBE ribbons."

The boat drew alongside, the seamen tossed their oars as though they were attending the naval review at Spithead, and the coxswain stood up in the sternsheets and saluted.

"Your engineer officer to repair aboard *Britannia*, Sir."

"Carry on, Chief." Haylestone ordered.

Once in the boat McNiff sat bolt upright beside the coxswain, his wispy hair floating in the breeze. "Heavy gulfweed, Sir," Haylestone heard the coxswain remark to his passenger, as they pulled away. And he heard the passenger's response. "Dang stuff covers the sea like a New England boiled dinner swamps a plate." Hiram Haylestone's confidence rose.

The captain and the mate waited on the bridge. Haylestone had urged the second engineer to clear the intake before McNiff returned and had sent a deck hand down to help him.

"Glad Angus went."

"He don't like boats," Quail observed.

"No. Angus spent too many days in an open boat during the war and damn nearly perished. He doesn't speak of it but I got it from a shipmate once who suffered with him."

They idly watched the cook come up to the back of the bridge and root about inside one of the lifeboats. He withdrew some poor looking carrots and collected a bucket of potatoes. Quail then turned his eyes to the yacht.

"Just to think . . . Angus hibernating with royalty!"

"Consorting, Merv."

"Consorting. He'll have his head turned proper, so spare-me-days!"

"If he does I'll turn it back for him."

Then they noticed figures getting into the boat. It moved towards them.

Alongside the *Maid* McNiff was assisted in his disembarkation from the whaler as though he were an admiral of the fleet. An officer in a white uniform followed him over the rail. He addressed the captain.

"Admiral Royal Yachts wishes to thank you for the services of your engineer officer."

"He's welcome."

"You're bound for Nova Scotia?"

"Yes. Halifax."

"Direct?"

Haylestone hesitated. But it was only a momentary pause while he glanced across at the *Britannia.*

"Direct."

"What is your estimated time of arrival at Halifax, Captain Haylestone?"

"Well, let's see now . . . " He pulled gently at the point of his beard. "What's the date today?"

"December the thirteenth."

The captain examined some fleecy clouds in an otherwise blue sky. "Thirteen hundred miles . . . at ten knots . . . "

"Nine knots," McNiff interrupted.

"Ten knots with the current contrary . . . six days. Say a week. That'll be the twentieth."

"Captain Haylestone." The officer spoke deliberately but with charm. "You are commissioned to carry a diplomatic pouch to the Lieutenant Governor of Nova Scotia for onward transmission to the Governor General of Canada. It is important that it reaches the residency in Ottawa by Christmas Day. You obviously have ample time. Thank you, Sir."

The officer spoke to the coxswain of the boat who passed up a small satchel, bound with a red tape and sealed. He delivered it to Haylestone and saluted.

"Honour, I'm sure." Haylestone executed a kind of bow and his visitor departed.

Much speculation and debate went on after that. What did the diplomatic pouch contain? Some important document if it was being delivered by hand. But someone said all royal documents were carried by hand. However, it was generally concluded that Christmas greetings were among the contents, and possibly a Christmas gift.

McNiff spoke in high praise of their treatment of him. He had fixed the pump himself, a tricky but simple job, under the professional eyes of an engineer in a brass hat, and several lesser lights. Then he delivered a lecture on its peculiar operation. He wound up in some mess-room where he had two very large tots of grog and a cup of tea, during which, he said, he had been asked questions by an officer as to the *Maid's* destination and date of arrival. They had then given him the pouch and instructions but he had protested because he was fearful of dropping it in the ditch. So it was decided that an officer would deliver it to the captain.

"Just as well you didn't know our immediate destination," Haylestone snorted.

"What do you mean?"

"I mean we're going to East Jeddore first. But I wasn't going to tell the officer that. We can't go into Halifax until we've unloaded enough cargo to bring those blasted Plimsoll marks clear of the water. You ought to have enough common sense to know that, Angus."

McNiff fell silent.

"I'll get the stuff trucked to Halifax from East Jeddore. That's why I stuck on an extra day and made it a week."

Well north of Bermuda the sky became overcast and a long high swell drove up. It was dark before twilight and the heavy mainsail which had been steadying the vessel blew out just after supper in a squall. Then the wind came hard out of the northwest.

In the first watch Haylestone had to heave the *Maid* to. And so she remained for two days and three nights of storm. In the shrieking gale powerful waves rolled her down on her beam-ends to leeward and swept her clean as she staggered up. Her wallowing instability tore the nerves of the crew and her load was straining her hull. The main pump clogged often with sticky cargo seepage. At one precarious moment Haylestone admitted that the centre of buoyancy was probably in the wrong place and wished he were back in the lighter lobster trade; but he showed no weakening of command.

The din lessened and the tumult on deck subsided at dawn on the third day. The sun struggled out in mid-morning between rifts in the scudding clouds, and hope revived. The gale had blown itself out leaving only the ruts in the road. But the effect of the onslaught, like the wages of sin, would be costly.

It was the twenty-first when they got underway again, and in the two days that followed the stress of deciding between East Jeddore and the Lieutenant Governor told on Haylestone's temper. He visualized the dreadful embarrassment of the Governor General of the Dominion trying to word an overdue radio message of thanks for greetings and gifts received by courtesy of the tardy Captain Hiram Haylestone of the *Maid of Jeddore*. McNiff would certainly not get a medal – just as well.

It was as though a shackle had been knocked out of his heart when on the twenty-third the tall tower of Sambro Light appeared over the horizon. But now . . . which port? Play it safe . . . or serve the Crown? A quick calculation showed he could not take the sure course; there was no time to deviate. He would attempt to squeeze into Halifax unnoticed. The *Maid* stood on.

But her berth was occupied when she arrived in the middle of the afternoon. Haylestone was obliged to anchor. And the anchorage he was forced to take was directly opposite the lofty tower of the Department of Transport building. Haylestone chewed up cigars faster than he smoked them. And he had no lifeboat to go ashore as a royal courier should without delay – both boats had been swept overboard in the gale.

After dark they came alongside. The port warden himself was there to greet the trader from the Lesser Antilles, and Haylestone saw him from the bridge playing the beam of his powerful flashlight on the vessel's side as she came to the wharf.

The small satchel, bound with the scarlet tape and sealed, lay on a heap of blankets on the captain's bunk in the little cabin abaft the wheel-house. Haylestone was pulling on his overcoat when the port warden thumped up the ladder and came in. There were no preliminaries.

"Captain Hiram Haylestone. I regret very much that I find one of our own coastal skippers, renowned for serving this port for many years," his voice dropped " – renowned in more ways than one – loading his vessel in a way no other local master would, disregarding the rules of the Department of Transport, disregarding the laws of safety at sea, disregarding the . . . the authority of the port warden of the Port of Halifax." The officer's voice had risen again. "This will mean suspension, seizure of your vessel until your fine, levied by the inches that the vessel is below her marks, is paid. You're in trouble my friend."

Haylestone felt like McNiff must have done when told to take to an open boat. He had taken a chance and lost. And he knew he was unprepared for his defence. The *Maid of Jeddore* was great in her pregnancy, she showed it and could not deny it.

The captain sat down. He was still in his overcoat. "It's time I bought that farm, I guess," he said, half to himself, staring out the door into the dim wheel-house.

"You'll have no money for a farm after you've bailed yourself out of this mess, if you ever do. Farming in the pen perhaps."

Suddenly there was a sound of pounding feet. The wheel-house door banged and in a flash a half-dressed man staggered into the cabin. It was Angus McNiff.

He was in an undershirt, his best blue trousers (sagging) and his yellow shore-going shoes. Trailing from one hand were what seemed to be a pair of grimy pants, and in the other he held a bedraggled envelope having a curious bend to it.

"Here, Hiram, take it," he croaked, puffing. He brushed the port warden aside as he burst in. "I found it in the arse pocket of my working pants. Forgot it was there." He was speaking hurriedly between short gasps. "I remember it being given me . . . aboard the royal yacht. I shoved it in my pocket and never thought of it again. Don't use my arse pocket normally. These are the pants." He held the wrinkled atrocities up. Haylestone recognized them without difficulty. "Fetching them ashore to be washed. Always look through the pockets first; automatic like."

Haylestone had torn the heavy envelope open. His dark eyes scanned the crested sheet bent to the shape of McNiff's buttocks. Then he rose massively to his feet, like a rocket slowly lifting off its pad, and brought his heavy black whiskers within a foot of the port warden's face.

"I and the *Maid of Jeddore* have diplomatic immunity. Neither you nor the DOT can touch me. Here, read this." He thrust the emblazoned document under the nose of the port warden.

"I shall now take this pouch to Government House on Barrington Street," he said majestically, picking up the colourful satchel from among the blankets, "for onward transmission to the Governor General – if it isn't too bloody late."

Captain Hiram Haylestone crammed his best civilian hat on, flicked the document from the port warden's hand and stuffed it in his pocket.

"Thanks, Angus," he said, thumping him on the back. "See you next week," he called back to the port warden as he went out the wheel-house door, "when my cargo is discharged. Merry Christmas to you."

# Scuttling

The passage from Yarmouth to Boston was trying for Captain Hiram Haylestone. To begin with, the *Maid of Jeddore* was only half loaded: the Nova Scotia apples which he had contracted to carry had suffered a blight and much of the harvest was not good enough to export. This was particularly distressing when cargoes generally were plentiful. To make matters more dismal, the engine broke down when they were hardly past the Lurcher Shoal.

Angus McNiff said it was the age of the diesel, it needed taking down and rebuilding. Haylestone questioned that; he was familiar with the chief's pessimistic appraisal of a mechanical failure. After drifting like a log of pulp wood for two hours in the strong tide out of the Bay of Fundy, the captain descended to the engine room to give him encouragement.

McNiff, with a large spanner in his hand, was on his toes reaching over the big cylinder head, the seat of his oily pants so low that his legs looked even shorter than usual. The configuration reminded Haylestone of the rear view of a rock-hopping penguin he had once seen examining a boulder in the Arctic.

"What the hell are you doing there, Angus, playing the fiddle?" His voice echoed in the silent grotto. "Show me the trouble."

McNiff lit on his heels. "Can't, it's inside."

"What's the matter with the insides?"

"Piston's seized up."

"You're probably seized up yourself – with apple cider. Potent brew. I'll give you half an hour."

Repairs were eventually completed and the journey resumed, but soon Ambrose discovered a leak in the hull, though it was not severe.

"Rot," said McNiff who had to operate his bilge pump at frequent intervals. "Planks rotting."

This incensed Haylestone to the point where he actually threatened to fire the chief engineer when they got home.

It was an irksome voyage.

Haylestone was on the Boston dock watching his cargo being discharged. The crates were in good order, the leak had obviously not blemished the apples. Standing there he was the image of strength, one who would give way to nothing, either physically or morally, a veritable master of the sea. It was this aspect of the captain of the *Maid of Jeddore* that made the stranger who was approaching him do so with vigilance. The man was of modest height, stout, and carried himself erectly as men do who have to hold up their stomachs.

"Cap'n Haylestone?" he questioned huskily out of one side of his mouth – a cigar was fastened to the other side.

"Yeah," Haylestone retorted.

"Glad to know you."

"You don't as far as I know."

"My name's Alonzo Baroni. I'm in business in Boston and Baltimore." He thrust out a pudgy hand with a big ring on one finger which Haylestone looked at and then reluctantly grasped, to Mr. Baroni's discomfort. But he recovered quickly.

"You been operating this boat a long time, Cap. You carry on a good trade." Baroni had a gravelly voice that sounded as though it came from a lower region than his throat.

"Who told you?"

"I have friends who know many people." He pushed back his hat revealing greying black curly hair. "The proprietor of the Ship Tavern said you was a good Nova Scotia skipper, carried anything."

"What about it?"

The intruder grinned. "Very interesting," he said.

"Mr . . . "

"Alonzo Baroni. Good American name."

"Mr. Baroni. What is it you want? And don't box the compass telling me."

Alonzo Baroni looked up at the giant whose pointed beard jutted down at him like a martingale boom. He knitted his thick brows and his eyes became brown beads.

"I got valuable freight I want transported. Very valuable freight. Be glad to ship it with you."

"Oh. What is it? Gold?"

"Wish it was." Baroni coughed roughly. "Computers."

"Computers? Where do you want me to take computers?"

"Oh, let's say, Jamaica."

Haylestone eyed the bronzed man of business whose thick nose, he felt sure, must at one time have been attacked by a hornet. "Why Jamaica?"

"University in Jamaica, ain't there?"

After a few moments silence Haylestone said, "You don't sound that particular about the freight's destination."

"I'm particular all right."

"Where is the cargo?"

"Baltimore."

"There's regular freighter service out of Baltimore to the Caribbean. Why don't you ship your stuff on a United States vessel?"

"Cap, them ships are too big. I like small ones. That's why I come to you. You been travelling them parts plenty. You know the score."

Haylestone grunted. "What's the rig?" he said sharply.

Baroni broke out a smile again. "What's the rig?" He looked up and down the dock and then at the captain. "My valuable cargo will be fully insured. Guess your boat is insured proper. I'll pay you plenty of freightage. Sink your boat and the cargo and we'll hit the jack pot – both of us."

"Mr. Baloney . . . "

"Baroni, Alonzo. Al if you like."

The captain's voice rose. "Sink . . . Sink my boat! Never heard the likes." Haylestone's massive moustache twitched. He leaned down towards his adversary, "Get out of my sight."

Under the fierce glare of the speaker any ordinary man would have made his escape rapidly. But Alonzo Baroni was obviously an unusual fellow; perhaps he had encountered other ferocious types during his years in business. He removed the cigar from his gilt teeth and cracked that blasted smile.

"Surely, Cap, ten or twenty thousand bucks would be a good return for taking the cargo. And your boat," he pointed a bent finger towards the *Maid of Jeddore,* "it looks old. You could get a new one. Your insurance and a government grant probably."

Activity on the dock had ceased; it was lunch hour. Baroni was now saying he had made a few deals in his time and they had always been successful – for both parties. He outlined one briefly in which he and his client had shared the excise tax. Suddenly he tabled his motion again. "What you say, Boss?"

Captain Haylestone had been looking up to heaven as though searching for a breeze to fill his sails. He may have seen a fleecy cloud in the blue celestial expanse for he came down to Baroni's level at about the moment the question was put.

"What do I say? What more have you to offer?"

Baroni's serious expression lit up. "I'll tell you. You got a boat, I got a shipment. Lose them both and we'll have a mite more working capital. I pays by the job." He spoke out of the farthest corner of his mouth this time, a corner, Haylestone suspected, he reserved for quoting figures. "Ten grand," he added. "Ten thousand dollars."

As the sea climbs and falls, relents and recoils, so Haylestone's mind sometimes curled and broke, and with the same generating force: the winds of chance.

He took a few paces to the edge of the wharf and stared down at the tide below. After a while he lifted his head and turned round.

"You said ten or twenty thousand just now."

"Ten or twenty? Did I?"

"You did. I'll say thirty."

"Thirty grand! That's big dough."

"Big job."

"Too much."

"Sure isn't. For losing my vessel to sink your bloody computers!"

"Very high price just the same."

"Got to compensate for inflation. You heard of inflation?"

"Big dough."

Haylestone looked out across the water. Presently he said simply, "Come back tomorrow."

With that he left the man with the good American name and strode towards his vessel.

Haylestone had time to think.

The *Maid of Jeddore* was indeed growing old; she leaked and the engine showed signs of fatigue. With the shipping business flourishing as it was, it would be more profitable to have a larger vessel, say a four-hundred ton steel ship, instead of a little wooden double-ender. Haylestone had thought of that a number of times in recent months.

The *Maid* was adequately insured, he had always seen to that. She had done well. It would be sad to part with her but sentimentality had no place in business. Or had it? There was his crew; none better. But he could take them to a bigger ship.

Was this the right thing to do? He spent a restless night thinking about it. Well, he had paid a great many insurance premiums, hadn't he, and made few claims? He had played his part with the *Maid of Jeddore*, upholding the traditions of the sea and serving his nation in an honourable profession.

Haylestone felt edgy nevertheless. In the morning, he walked out of his cabin into the sunlit wheelhouse, put a massive hand on a spoke of the wheel and gazed out of the window. The men working the cargo on the foredeck gradually dissolved, and he saw instead a slim, sparsely-clad damsel scampering forward into the arms of a film producer. His eyes became lucent. He saw a white racing yacht with her bow wedged in the mooring bits and a bull moving aft, head down, horns like marline spikes. And then the picture of the deceased Miss Scantelbury laid out under a tropical sun on that very hatch rose to his mind.

Those were great days, exciting days, with hardly a worry in the world . . .

His pleasant reverie was interrupted by someone puffing up the ladder. Hiram Haylestone's heart never sank but this time it acted like the first few strokes of McNiff's bilge pump before it sucked water. The promoter incarnate reached the top step and had a spasm of coughing. When it died down they withdrew to the captain's cabin.

"Hope you're agreeable, Cap," Alonzo Baroni opened wheezily.

"Yep," Haylestone answered abruptly. "Give me the gen."

Baroni outlined it: load the computers at Baltimore and sail for Jamaica: make away with the boat at the captain's discretion before reaching same but, since Baroni was coming along too to see fair play, it should be at a convenient location for survival without risk.

Haylestone quite agreed with the survival aspect, that was essential; nor did he want to be rescued by helicopter or any such perilous method. But he did not take to the proposal that Baroni accompany him.

"You question my honesty, Baroni? My integrity?"

"Matter of business principle," Baroni protested, spreading his hands. "Man's got to watch his investments."

"Ocean's cold, you know."

"I've bathed at Cape Cod."

After a rousing discussion Haylestone agreed but demanded that Baroni ship as the supercargo. "Can't take passengers. No licence for that."

"Okay," said Baroni, "it's all the same."

"I'll settle for cash, now. Thirty thousand. And then you pay me the standard freightage at Baltimore to regularize the transport of the cargo."

From a hidden pocket the man from Boston and Baltimore pulled out a wad of bills such as Haylestone had never seen. But he said he didn't have enough. He counted out eleven thousand and said he would go ashore and get the rest.

Haylestone's bad temper crept on him soon after Baroni had left. Even the banking of the final payment of nineteen thousand did not bring the contentment it should have. Sailing down the coast he realized it was with himself that he was annoyed, and by the time the *Maid of Jeddore* had made Chesapeake Bay he knew he had undertaken something that, had he had the sense of a common horsefly, he would have avoided biting.

What powers had this character possessed that he could have oiled the bearings of Haylestone's honest mind with such an evil lubricant that his thinking for a short but fatal term had run smoothly down into the maelstrom? In a bout of remorse he felt more worthy to be the bearer of a millstone than the master of the *Maid of Jeddore*, that lovable child of the high seas. But now he had taken her across the Rubicon and had reached the port of Baltimore.

Baroni was there on the dock with two vans. A number of heavy packing cases were unloaded which the mate and his men hoisted aboard and stowed in the fore hold well forward in the usual manner so that they could work backwards as successive consignments arrived. As the empty vans drove away, Haylestone noticed that there was no identifying name on them. They certainly did not look as if they came from I.B.M.

They returned later with one more shipment but that was all.

"Where's the rest of the cargo?" the captain wanted to know.

Seated in Haylestone's cabin, Alonzo Baroni peered into his breast pocket and pulled out a cigar. "There ain't no more, Cap. You got your load."

"That's hardly twenty tons, not ten per cent of my capacity."

"What's wrong with that?"

"I'm in the habit of sailing with a full cargo."

"Why do you want a full cargo when you're going to sink it anyway?"

"Oh . . . Yeah." It was his trader's instinct.

"Bill of lading," Baroni announced, pulling out of his pocket a number of copies of a large form and spreading them out on the captain's desk. "Needs signing."

Haylestone, used to the type of document, glanced over the filled-in spaces; then he thrust his head closer.

"Value, one million, eight hundred thousand dollars! Too many noughts. One thousand, eight hundred they mean."

"They don't. Computers are worth more than peanuts."

"One million, eight hundred thousand! I can't carry that much. Not merchandise to that value."

"You got it, Cap."

"You should have shipped the damned things in a fast cargo liner, not a little double-ender."

"Ain't you forgetting something, Cap?" Baroni rasped.

Hiram Haylestone's ingrained propensity for thinking in the standard terms of "the safe and timely delivery of the cargo at its destination," made him forget for a moment that his freight had to be disposed of in an uncommon manner. He wondered if he was suffering from a malfunctioning memory. Having decided almost instantly that he was not, he turned to the obvious question of the freight rate, whether the stuff was going to Jamaica or to Davie Jones's locker.

With the stub of a pencil he worked it out on the back of his copy of the bill of lading and it did not come to much. So he applied half of one per cent of its value and said, "Nine thousand for freight."

Baroni's dark face contorted as though he had bitten on an exposed nerve of a tooth. "Nine what?"

"Nine thousand dollars. Cash now."

"You barmy?"

"Not that I know."

"Nine grand!" Baroni wiped his face with his handerchief. "You have no authority . . . "

"We agreed at Boston you'd pay the freight as well."

"Preposterous rate."

"The *Maid of Jeddore* is known for her safe delivery."

"Don't make me laugh."

"Got to charge high freightage to make it look proper when the day of judgement comes."

"That's a lot of hogwash."

"If you don't like it," Haylestone barked, "I'll unload your bloody machinery and you can take it home."

"Blackmail!" Baroni coughed, his hoarse voice becoming scratchier. "It's blackmail!"

The captain was on his feet. "Blackmail! Keep that for your own operations Mr. Baloney. Take it or leave it. Nine thousand or I'll unload."

Baroni gazed up at the weather-beaten face, then studied the planks of the cabin deck. Presently he pushed himself up from the settee with his hands and aimed for the door. "I'll be back," he half groaned.

He was, within an hour. All Haylestone had to do now was to transfer the cash to his bank in Halifax.

Baroni wanted to know exactly how the captain was going to do the "job" before he sailed as supercargo, also when and where. Haylestone's estimates of the latter were rough, and it was evident that the islands in the Caribbean he spoke of so glibly were only vaguely known to Baroni. They might have lain off Patagonia.

As to the "job," Haylestone told Baroni he would explain it to him tonight when he came aboard ready to sail first thing in the morning. Then he made an unexpected request. "Can you get me half a dozen tickets for the ball game this evening?"

"Ball game? Why, sure. Course I can. I'll send them down by messenger this aft."

Captain Hiram Haylestone knew his vessel as Angus McNiff knew his engine – probably better – and it was in the light of this familiarity that he worked out his operational stratagem. And having done so he felt much better. There was challenge in the air now – albeit a rather unusual one. The first thing he did after midday dinner was to call the mate up to his cabin. When Quail was comfortably seated on the bunk and had his pipe kindled, Haylestone began to break the news.

"Merv, you and I have sailed together for many years. How many I wonder?" His voice was almost tender. "Seven in the *Maid of Jeddore* and a good few before that, eh? You know me or ought to by this time, and I know you, among other fine qualities, to be a reticent fellow."

"Ret . . . ?"

"Silent, Merv."

Merv took the soliloquy as though he had heard something like it before.

"You've always done what I've wanted; you've always been loyal. Would you stand by me in any circumstances?"

Merv didn't answer, not that that meant a negative response.

"I know you would, Merv. But these circumstances are rather abnormal, so to speak. You've seen this guy, Alonzo Baloney . . . Baroni who's been coming to see me? He wants me to sink his cargo."

Merv grasped his pipe with his fist so that he could release his teeth from the stem preparatory to speaking. "Sink? Sink his cargo? How? Throw it overboard?"

"No. Goes down with the ship."

"Crazy coot." Quail scrutinized his pipe and put it back in his mouth.

"It could be done."

"Who the hell's going to do a thing like that there?"

"I am," Haylestone said quietly.

Quail fell back. "What! You going to . . . to . . . "

"Stand fast, Merv. Listen. We're taking these high priced computers to Jamaica. Mighty high priced. We get down near to an island, say San Salvador or Crooked Island in the Bahamas, before reaching the Windward Passage anyway, and pull the plugs out of her and take to the boats. And . . . "

"Boats!"

"Boats. And when the *Maid* sinks we'll hoist sail and make for the land with a fair trade wind."

Quail sat up straight. "You . . . you gone crazy, Hiram? Spare-me-days, you ain't serious!"

"I am. And you've got to help me."

"What for are you doing it?"

"Insurance – and high compensation."

"They'll catch you, Hiram."

"No they won't."

"By jeeze!" Merv was standing up. "Scuttle the

*Maid of Jeddore*?" He seemed to be mesmerized. "Sink her! She's good. She's too good to lose. 'Sides, Hiram, it's wrong."

Haylestone could see Merv was almost beside himself. He reached into the locker under the settee and fished out a bottle. With one hand holding its neck he put the other on Merv's shoulder. "Get your arse down onto the bunk. You need a dose of tonic."

Merv had no alternative.

After he had swallowed half a glass of neat Schreecher's in three quick draughts, Haylestone resumed his elucidation.

"Merv, I'm depending on you to see me through. Don't spill the tar – you wouldn't anyway. Only other person who'll know will be Baloney. He's coming with us."

"Coming with us!"

"All hands except you and me will be at the ball game this evening. You don't like baseball, see. When all are ashore we'll rig the vessel for the job."

"How?"

"You got an auger in the locker for'ard?"

"Auger? Yeah."

"Bring it aft when they've gone."

"By cripes, not that!" Merv Quail stared incredulously at Haylestone, then quickly drank the rest of his rum.

"It's okay, Merv. You just rely on me."

"Rely . . . " After seeming to think he said, "Get Angus onto it."

"Not Angus. No. You, Merv. Angus will be ashore. That's where I want him."

Quail wanted to know what would happen if Angus McNiff decided not to go to the ball game.

"I think he will. If he doesn't, I'll give him this bottle; it's half full."

"Ugh. Maybe need more than that," Quail surmised.

"Well, we'll put a squirt of tranquilizer into it, same as we use for bulls and heifers; I still have some. That'll flatten old Nosy McNiff."

But McNiff was spared; he was happy to go to the game.

When the coast was clear, Haylestone called Quail who was pacing the quay. The boat apparently did not provide him with enough space to work off his nervous energy. He told him to fetch the auger aft, and a hammer and saw and the wooden plugs he had asked him to make. They took the covers off the after hatch, Quail lifting them with the slow deliberation of a longshoreman working to rule, connected a light to a wandering lead and went down into the hold.

Haylestone cut out a section of the inner skin to get at the thick timbers.

"Where do you figure the water line is, Merv?" he asked.

"Don't know."

"You can guess as well as I can," Haylestone barked.

Quail measured with his eye downwards from the deck above, but did not volunteer his estimate. Haylestone did the same but he had to be exact. He told Quail to go up and tap the hull with the hammer just above the water. Haylestone listened with a stethoscopic ear and determined where the water line was. He put the auger against the ship's side about a foot below it and began drilling.

After a time he stopped and blew the shavings out of the hole. "You have a go, Merv."

"I don't hold with it, Hiram." Reluctance sounded in every word.

"I know you don't. You've said as much before but that needn't stop you from boring a simple two-inch hole."

"It do."

"Merv. You damn well get onto the auger and turn it."

Merv Quail still hesitated.

Haylestone felt exasperation bearing down on him. The mate's obstinacy suddenly reminded him of his near mutiny once when he refused to shift some gravestones in the fore hold during a storm. A hard line had to be adopted, he could see that. He leaned forward, the auger in his hand.

"I'm the master of this vessel, you're the mate – the chief officer. The laws of the sea demand that the crew obey the master, particularly the officers, and more particularly the chief officer." Quail had moved back. "It's your duty to do what I tell you. Take the matter up as a complaint against the captain in your home port if you like, Mervin Quail." His voice was low, hard, and clear.

The mate grasped the auger as though it was a limpet bomb and slowly inserted it in the hole. The honest Quail, by nature faithful to his captain, true to the ethics of the sea, had unbent. "Obey now, complain later, Mervin Quail"; the credit card philosophy had probably done it.

He was soon leaning heavily on the auger and the twisting was hard. The bit was through the spruce timbers and was biting into the outer greenheart ice skin. At this point they went up on deck and lowered the weighted hatch tarpaulin down into the water and flat against the side like an apron. "That'll stop the water pouring in when we bore right through," Haylestone said. "The navy call it a collision mat; blocks up the hole when they ram one another. Navy's always colliding."

Water only trickled in when the hole was completed, and when they had driven a long plug in and removed the tarpaulin, the *Maid* was as tight as ever.

They bored another hole in the same way on the other side to make sure the sea would enter the hold quickly.

"Leave the hatch covers off, Merv," Haylestone said when they came up. "Got to show Baloney our art work."

"Yours," Merv rejoined.

Alonzo Baroni was aboard with his suitcase before the baseball fans returned and at once demanded to know how the captain was going to sink the ship; by opening the sea-cocks he supposed.

"Sea-cocks! What are they?" Haylestone asked derisively. "Some new kind of Watergate?"

"Sea-cocks. Things you open up to let the sea in."

"What for? Oh yeah. Come to think of it I've read of sea-cocks in stories or the papers. But I'll show you something that'll pass for a couple. They're Haylestone sea-cocks." The captain actually laughed.

At some risk he got Baroni to climb down the ladder to the hold and with the lamp showed him the long-handled plugs sticking out of the ship's side. "Just pull them out and there you are," he explained.

Alonzo Baroni was satisfied. When he came up on deck there was a smile on his face that resembled that of an arsonist who has just made doubly sure that he has his matches with him.

The *Maid of Jeddore* performed very well on the voyage south except for the leak. She was logging nine knots against a moderate south-east wind when she passed Cape Hatteras but she would soon fall in with the favourable trades. The sunny trip, however, was rather marred by what modernists would call the behavior syndrome of the personnel.

Alonzo Baroni, who had bedded down in the messroom, was a nuisance to the crew. He was untidy and remained more or less recumbent except when he went to the lee rail – and sometimes by mistake to the weather rail. He had apparently forgotten that a boat has to adjust herself to the bumpiness of the sea. He gave up cigars and ate nothing but hardtack. Angus McNiff took umbrage from the beginning because Baroni chose to stretch out on the settee next to where the chief normally sat for his meals. McNiff treated him as though he were a parasite and after a good many recriminatory conversations declined to speak to him at all.

McNiff was troubled about Merv Quail too. He spoke to the captain about it. "Goes about like he's in a trance. Don't speak to nobody. Burns more matches than tobacco; I told him he'd poison himself with match-head brimstone but he took no notice. Don't seem to hear right."

"Merv's okay, Angus," Haylestone assured the chief. "Quiet fellow, always."

"Quiet! He's deaf and dumb. Only thing he says to me in the three days since we left Baltimore, when I happened to mention my engine was pushing her along good, was, 'You might as well run your danged engine hard and wear it out.' That ain't like Merv, Hiram."

"Merv's all right," Haylestone said again. He threw the stump of his cigar over the side and watched the white gulls gliding gracefully over the vessel on their pale grey wings.

"I'm worried, Hiram."

"You worry too much. Merv's probably overpowered a bit by the supercargo."

"That Alonzo guy!" McNiff kicked the stanchion in front of him then winced. "You got to be careful of that plug ugly, Hiram. Wouldn't trust him a fathom under water. Don't know what you hired him for. There's only a pocketful of cargo and you could look after that as well as him.

"Don't bother with Baloney."

"Plug ugly," McNiff went on. "I'll let you know, Hiram, if I get a drift of any dirty work from that quarter."

"Thanks, Angus. Harmless guy really, though he doesn't look it."

"He sure don't. And I think you're right. Merv's affected by him. Cook too. He's mad. You got him started when you made him take his spuds and veges out of the lifeboat."

Haylestone grunted. "You get down to your dungeon and forget about people."

Haylestone was not worried about anyone; he knew how each felt. As for himself, he was perfectly happy. He encountered Baroni squatting on the bottom step of the bridge ladder outside the galley taking gasps of fresh air as though suffering from some lung complaint.

"Feeling better?"Haylestone inquired kindly.

"Bit," he answered. He looked up and Haylestone saw a pair of frightened eyes. "How do people escape a sinking ship?"

After a moment's hesitation Haylestone said, "Boats, of course."

"B-boats? Us too?"

Haylestone's sympathy was strained. "Quiet, you idiot."

"Call another ship and take us off."

"My sainted aunt! Don't throw boomerangs at it and muck it up," he muttered sharply.

"I wish I hadn't . . . "

"Pipe down. I'll drop you off at a nice Hilton hotel first."

The captain strode off making the deck ring more than usual.

Late in the afternoon of the fourth day they sighted San Salvadore and by dusk had the northern end of the island abeam to port. The captain adjusted his course slightly making due allowance for the set and drift of the current and ordered the chief engineer to reduce his revs to give eight knots instead of ten. McNiff thought this extraordinary; he had never known the captain go slower than full out in good weather in the open ocean. More people were becoming eccentric.

But Haylestone did not want to reach Crooked Island Passage before dawn. It was a moonless night so he did not see Rum Cay.

When Quail came onto the bridge to relieve the captain at four o'clock he looked, by the light of the binnacle, as if he had spent a sleepless watch below. Haylestone gave him the course being steered, as usual, and told him to call him if he saw the flash of the lighthouse on Bird Rock. He entered a note in the log book, "Course south by east, approaching Crooked Island." He fell asleep on his bunk quickly.

Crooked Island came over the horizon fine on the port bow soon after sunrise and the captain held his course. The trade wind picked up from the east-north-east as the sun gained height. Before seven he quietly told the mate to go down the after hold with a flashlight, taking care not to disturb the chief while he was removing the locking bars, and pull out both plugs. "We left the hammer down there, you remember, to help knock them out. Batten the hatch down after."

Quail hesitated. Haylestone saw his distress.

"Hiram. It's terrible, so spare-me-days. I won't be able to live with it."

Haylestone grasped the mate's arm. "Merv, old fellow, remember what I said, have confidence in me. And I'm forcing you to do this. You won't be found at fault."

"You ain't President Nixon, are you?"

"A shipmaster is safer than a president."

Quail hung his head, shuffled down the ladder slowly and went aft.

By eight the *Maid of Jeddore* entered the passage between Crooked Island, now a mile or so to port, and Long Island, twenty-five miles to starboard, and ceased her heavy rolling. Quail approached the captain in the port wing of the bridge. The weather door of the wheel-house was shut.

"Where you doing it, Hiram?" he almost whispered.

Haylestone glanced at the low-lying island, then at his watch. "Down the coast a bit I reckon. Angus starts his small pump about now but he'll find it won't suck her dry. Go down to breakfast, Merv."

Quail looked at the rippled water between the boat and the tree-fringed sandy shore. "Never reach that island under sail; dead beat to windward. Row maybe, but current's strong. What's to leeward?"

"Long Island just over the horizon."

"Why not run down and get closer to it?"

"Want the calm water that's under this island. Get your breakfast."

"Don't want none."

"Look better if you did. Soon as you've finished send Elmer to sound the bilges for'ard."

Presently the engine room voice pipe whistled. McNiff wanted to report the leak seemed worse and he was changing over to his big pump.

When Elmer took the sounding he wiped the rod off and dropped it down the pipe a second time. Then he shouted up to the bridge. "Sixteen inches in the bilges, Skipper."

"Sixteen?"

"Yeah. Sixteen."

"Sound her aft, Elmer."

He reported four inches aft. Haylestone told him to stand by on the fore deck and sound every ten minutes.

Merv Quail's breakfast did not take long. He glanced into both boats on his way to the bridge.

The water was gaining. In thirty minutes the two foot mark had been passed. Haylestone looked at the boats then at the shore and stepped into the wheel-house. He put the telegraph to slow speed and blew down the engine room tube. "Angus, she's leaking bad," he shouted. "Run both pumps."

"Better start the hand pump, Hiram," said Quail. "Them computers'll be getting wet some."

"Doesn't matter. Yeah. Put a hand on the pump just the same."

When Elmer reported four feet of water for'ard the captain went into the wheel-house and rang down "stop."

"Merv," he shouted as he came out, "muster all hands on deck. Open up the fore hatch." His voice carried to every corner of the vessel except possibly the engine room where the pumps were pounding away.

Elmer dropped his sounding rod at the emergency call and was joined almost at once by an off-watch hand who had the bars off and the tarpaulin back in moments. The captain and the mate went down,

Elmer and Ambrose following, and found themselves knee deep at the foot of the ladder and looking at water gurgling over the sunken treasure.

"Shine your light on the ship's side, Merv" – Haylestone was conscious of witnesses. "Dry . . . dry as the cook's bread. Might be in the fore peak but we can't get at it. Up the ladder now," he ordered, displaying the need for haste.

He found everyone on deck except McNiff. He was sent for and on his arrival Hiram Haylestone addressed his crew.

"She's taking water fast and the pumps can't keep up with it. We've got to abandon ship. Lower the boats and board them soon as they're in the water. You take the starboard boat, Merv, with the second engineer, cook, and two seamen. I'll take you, Angus, the supercargo, and the other two men. Stop your pumps, Angus. Now, get to it."

As they were dispersing he added, "Angus, hold my boat till I've sent an S.O.S."

He went up to his cabin and switched on the radio telephone. There would be no excuse if he did not call for help. The ether was soundless but he wished he had done some listening earlier. He squeezed the transmitter and spoke rapidly.

"*Maid of Jeddore, Maid of Jeddore*. Calling all ships. S.O.S., S.O.S., S.O.S. Leaking badly. Vessel sinking. About to abandon ship. Position two miles west of Crooked Island. Hope to sail life-boats to Long Island. S.O.S., S.O.S., *Maid of Jeddore*. Out."

He waited for about a minute and was relieved to hear nothing. He switched off and went out – to hear lusty local utterances. McNiff's voice was uppermost, sounding as if he was grappling with a carnivorous quadruped on the South African veldt.

"Get your bloody carcass into the boat or I'll throw you in!"

The loud reply was "No."

"Plug ugly, you don't have to be an Olympic hurdler to get down there."

"Leave me alone. Life-boat's too small."

The captain hove in sight. "What the hell are you talking about, Baloney? Down into the boat with you."

Alonzo Baroni had one fat leg over the bulwark rail, which McNiff was holding, having apparently got it that far, and was flailing his arms in the evident hope of making fast to a stanchion or something that would prevent him going further. "Can't go," he whined. "Cap, stop the ship sinking."

He reminded Haylestone of a petrified heifer baulking at the gangway. "Can't, you fool. Jump over and don't fall in the ditch."

"My fault," he cried in a low and broken tone.

"Shut your trap," roared Haylestone.

"Run her ashore and we'll climb out."

"Couldn't get within two cables of the beach. She'd go aground in the surf."

"Well, do something else."

Haylestone closed like a wrestler. "Seize his other leg, Angus. Heave-ho. Catch him Ambrose."

It was like disposing of jetsam.

But Angus wasn't finished. "Hang on, Hiram, I'll get a few bottles of cordial; can't take to the boats without survival kit." He looked over the side. "Ed, climb back up and give me a hand."

"Stay where you are, Ed." Haylestone commanded and turned on the chief. "No rum in the boat."

"You gone crackers, Hiram? Cast away like this without . . . "

"Angus." Haylestone was bellowing now. "I said no rum. Get aboard the life-boat this instant or I'll go without you."

McNiff had not sailed with his captain all these years without knowing the significance of that bellow. He unwillingly went over the rail and jumped down, closely followed by Haylestone.

They pulled away. The mate's boat had already come around the stern and was heading for the island under oars. The captain's boat rowed some two hundred yards and stopped. Haylestone hailed the mate to come alongside.

They stayed close together resting on their oars. Quail expressed some concern about drifting away from Crooked Island. The two boats and the *Maid* were being set to leeward together by the wind and current. As the distance from the shore increased the boats began to rock.

The *Maid of Jeddore* was plainly on a very uneven keel. She was down about three feet by the head. After half an hour in comparative silence they thought she had sunk another foot for'ard. The stern was up a little.

The boats had not moved. All were watching the *Maid.* Baroni, seated in the stern sheets opposite the captain and holding the gunwale tightly, looked at her with malevolent eyes and at the sea as though he might very soon be eligible for the obituary columns of the *Baltimore Sun* and the *Boston Globe.* McNiff, automatically rolling a cigarette, told him he was sorry they hadn't any seat belts.

Neither sail was hoisted nor oars put out except when the mate's boat drifted out of earshot. Their distance from the vessel remained about the same; it provided the perspective Haylestone wanted; to all but him the *Maid* looked sad, forlorn, forsaken.

After an hour and a quarter the boats were shipping spray, being farther out into the passage. Haylestone called to Quail.

"She's not going down any more. What's your opinion?"

"Been about the same this last half hour," came the reply.

"What do you think, Angus?"

"By jeeze! She's holding up like you say."

"Leak must have stopped somehow," Haylestone observed.

"Must have. That's mighty curious."

There was silence for a while except for the ever-higher waves slapping against the weather sides of the boats. Then the captain cried, "We'll re-embark, Merv. I'll go alongside first." To his small crew he said, "Out oars, my boys."

They clambered aboard over the lee side and hoisted Baroni up. Haylestone beckoned Quail aside. "Get down the after hold quick and hammer the plugs in."

Then he shouted orders. "Start your pumps, Angus. Hoist the starboard boat, then take the port one round and hook her on. Cook, you and I'll go down the fore hold and inspect it."

No one took any notice of the supercargo.

Haylestone felt that he had convinced the cook that he had made an unproductive examination and came up to find Quail striking the palms of his hands across one another as though knocking off the dust of a dirty job, which reminded him of the account he had learned as a child in Sunday school about Pontius Pilate washing his hands. He went to the bridge, his favourite place of meditation, but did not have long to cogitate alone. Baroni worked his way up.

"Cap, what you going to do?" He looked like a member of the underworld who had just been informed by his banker that robbers had bored through the vault and made off with his safety deposit box. "When you going to put her under?"

"Thought you changed your mind just now."

"That was different. She's got to sink."

"She won't."

"But she must."

"She won't go down. Can't get her to. You can see that."

"You got to sink her. That was the deal. I got near forty grand tied up in her."

"If you'd put a full cargo of heavy computers into her as I expected she'd have gone down like a stone. But you elected to load only a wheelbarrow full so what can you expect?"

"It's your responsibility . . . "

"Hiram!" The shout came from Quail on the boat deck. "Ship in sight astern."

Haylestone glanced back. "By thunder!" he exclaimed and rushed into his cabin. Switching the radio on he cursed himself for not cancelling his S.O.S. sooner. He squeezed the transmitter.

"*Maid of Jeddore, Maid of Jeddore.* Calling all ships. Annul my S.O.S. Cancel my S.O.S. of two hours past. Have reboarded. Leak stopped, leak stopped. Pumps started again. Hope to hold it until we can make port. No casualties. Out."

He did not wait for an answer. He lept out and rang "stand by" on the engine room telegraph and when it was answered he put it to slow ahead. "She's too heavy for'ard for full speed," he breathed to Quail. "Well, if that's a fancy cruise ship she won't bother with us." He told Baroni to get below.

The ship astern gained quickly. Quail was watching her with the glasses.

"Hell, Hiram! She's the U.S. coast guard."

"No!" Haylestone exploded. "Let's have a look."

Quail handed him the binoculars.

"Did you replace the inner lining planks we pulled off?"

"Didn't have time."

"Well, nip down and saw the handles off the plugs – they'll still be sticking out – and replace the boards. Quick as you can now, Merv. Coast guard may be inquisitive."

The coast guard cutter was barrelling up with a bow wave that must have been costing the American taxpayer a dollar or two a second. "Here's a bloody circus," Haylestone murmured to himself. With a faint clanging of engine room bells she drew abreast of the *Maid.*

"Heard your signals. Brave work, Captain," came an encouraging voice from the cutter. "I'm sending over a pump to help you out." Haylestone protested; he was making out all right. But a whaler was already in the water and in a few minutes sailors were swarming aboard armed with hoses and hoisting up a big pump. The normal procedure of drawing the water out of the hold followed, McNiff going mad with indignation.

Perhaps for the sake of comradeship, or relief from boredom, or curiosity, the commander came aboard in a second boat. Haylestone was not overjoyed at his arrival but his greeting was somewhat more convivial than Stanley's when he ran into Livingstone. He led him into his cabin and opened the wine locker with the simplicity of a conjurer. He explained his predicament as being the stress placed by the severity of the north-east trades on a weak and leaking hull.

At the second sampling of the rum, for no understandable reason, Baroni appeared at the cabin door. Seeing the commander he backed off into the wheelhouse, trod on the collapsible stool which jumped up and seemed to frighten him, and disappeared below.

The commander was on his feet.

"Who's your man?"

"Supercargo."

"Name?"

"Why?"

"Is it . . . " he thought a moment. "Baroni?"

"It is."

"Thank you Captain. Most fortuitous."

"You know him?"

"Sure do. If you don't mind I'd like to relieve you of him."

"What for?"

"He's been wanted by the coast guard and other agencies for some time. Alfonso Sorento, alias Alonzo Baroni, conman, forger, sharp dealer on a grand scale. Hope he didn't swindle you."

"Me? Oh, no."

"Sorry if it's inconvenient but I'd be delighted to have him. I'll make out a warrant for his arrest. He's probably making a trip to be out of the country for a while."

"Yeah, I was coming round to thinking that myself." Haylestone expressed himself as believing that it was most likely his duty to release him.

They then drank to Canadian – American relations and the commander left. So did Alonzo Baroni.

When the coast guard cutter had disappeared over the horizon and the wet cases had been inspected, Captain Haylestone swung round and headed north.

It was one of those clear fall days when the *Maid of Jeddore* sailed into Halifax, the blue water of the harbour ruffled by a cool scented breeze. Haylestone had thought it judicious to put in to the first Canadian port available on his route, Liverpool, to test the mood of the insurers. A surveyor had checked the vessel over and, with the supporting evidence the captain had to offer, attributed the perilous condition in which they had found themselves to very doubtful timbers.

The pungent, pleasant odours of the heterogeneous cargoes that had passed over the Halifax wharf drifted into the mess-room while the captain and mate were having a quiet cup of tea. Haylestone was speaking of the immediate future.

"I'm going to put her on the slip and have the weak planks replaced and then refit her. Made a fair profit this trip so I can manage it. I'll sell the scrap iron that was supposed to be computers to my friend the gravestone importer. I think I'll have a radar installed too. Must get in touch with that salesman who jiggered up the compass that time, Bob somebody."

"That was Bob Doggett."

"Yeah, I must see Bob Doggett."

Quail was thinking. "Fair profit you said." He took his pipe out of his mouth. "When I saw daylight through them holes down there in the Bahamas, and then had to saw the ends off of them plugs, I figured it out. Just came to me like that there. You must have worked some kind of a deal, Hiram. You knew she wouldn't sink."

"I wouldn't have bored the holes where I did if I thought she'd sink. Down by the head a little as she was with the cargo, or even on an even keel, water was bound to run for'ard – no water-tight bulkheads, you know, and the flow was pretty free alongside the kelson. Yeah. I knew the holes would come clear of the water after a while. I wonder you didn't catch on sooner."

Merv Quail shook his head slowly. "Never thought of it."

"Nor did Baloney. Sorry I couldn't put you wise during the operation and save you from all your misery but I couldn't risk it, too much money involved."

The chief came in with a packet of mail. "Elmer's just back from the post office. Two or three letters for you, Hiram." He poured out a mug of tea.

Haylestone was idly glancing at the envelopes and telling McNiff to make out his list of engine defects for the overhaul when his speech trailed off at the sight of an envelope from the Marine Underwriters' Association. He hesitated, then slit it open with his thumb. He felt a little apprehensive but its contents raised his eyebrows.

"Jeeze! Fancy that now!" He held the letter and its attachment further away from his eyes then closed the distance.

"Says . . . listen to this Merv, Angus. Says here: 'The report submitted by the United States Coast Guard, substantiated by radio messages, states that you and your crew reboarded the *Maid of Jeddore* after having abandoned her in a sinking condition, and with the aid of the former's pumps saved your vessel from foundering . . . '"

"His bloody pumps!" exclaimed McNiff.

"Quiet, will you," Haylestone retorted loudly. "Goes on: 'A recent survey confirms a marked weakness in the hull structure. For this fearless act and the consequent avoidance of considerable financial loss, the Marine Underwriters' Association wishes to thank you and to express its appreciation further by awarding you $1,000.'"

"A thousand bucks!"

Merv Quail emitted a low whistle, an unusual sound for him.

McNiff's old brass lighter fell from his hand and splashed into his mug. "By cripes! A thousand . . . one grand! What you going to do with it, Hiram; split it around the crew?"

"Split it? No." Captain Hiram Haylestone leaned back in his chair and gazed at the catsup and pickle rack on the bulkhead. "No. Send it back to the Marine Underwriters and tell them to give it to the Seamen's Orphans' Benevolent Society."